LITTLE
SURE SHOT

LITTLE
SURE SHOT

MATT RALPHS

ANDERSEN PRESS

First published in Great Britain in 2023 by
Andersen Press Limited
20 Vauxhall Bridge Road, London SW1V 2SA, UK
Vijverlaan 48, 3062 HL Rotterdam, Nederland
www.andersenpress.co.uk

2 4 6 8 10 9 7 5 3 1

British Library Cataloguing in Publication Data available.

ISBN 978 1 83913 201 8

Printed and bound in Great Britain by Clays Ltd, Elcograf S.p.A.

For Annie

PART ONE

1

EARLY WINTER, 1865

I'm right on the edge. I always wait here a spell so I *feel* the change. On my skin. In my heart. Behind, a breeze slips through the chopped-down wheat stalks. Sounds like a sigh. Above, birds call to one another and the sun flies higher still in a wide blue sky. It don't feel like winter's on the way. Maybe it won't come this year.

I must be quiet as a mouse, so I take off my boots, put them on a tree stump – *and don't forget them on the way back like you usually do, Annie!* – and creep into the woods. The woods. My favourite place in the world.

After the open fields, everything here feels . . . closer, darker, mysteriouser. Out there is warm dirt and sharp stones. In here is cool moss and soft leaves that squidge between my toes. Chilly air makes my skin prickle and come out in goosebumps. I breathe deep the smell of mulch, mushrooms and tree sap.

Pa's taught me the trees. One glance at their bark patterns and leaf shape's all I need. 'Beech, aspen, oak, hickory, maple,' I murmur as I pass. Yellow-gold leaves drift down around me – the trees are shedding their summer clothes.

I stop to listen. Branches creak like our stable door. Leaves rustle like Ma's best dress. Somewhere, deep in the green, a woodpecker raps. But there's no sign of who I'm hunting. Not a whistle nor a footstep. But he's in here *some*where, I know it.

Ma laughed when I told her this, but I reckon, even though it's darker, I see better *in* the woods than *out*. Good enough to see that someone's kicked a path through that leaf drift over there . . . I sidle round the outside (you won't catch *me* leaving a trail) and head deeper into the woods, darn certain now that I'm on the right track.

I reach the creek where me and John sometimes net for crawfish. (John's my little brother. I'm five. He's four.) The bank is steep and deep. So's not to slip, I climb down slowly using the sticky-out tree roots to hold onto, then I jump over the water at the bottom. The mud on the opposite side feels slimy-delicious and turns my feet black.

Ah! Fresh boot prints, near where the water bubble-rushes through a narrow bit between some rocks. Keeping low and quiet like our barn cats when they're stalking rats, I follow the prints to the top of the sloping bank . . . and peer through the long grass.

Ahead is the fallen oak, with its roots all twisted and pointing every which way. And there's Pa, crouched behind its trunk, back towards me, with the stock of his Kentucky long rifle pressed into his cheek. He's totally still, like he's been frozen, then I hear the *snick* as he pulls back the rifle's hammer. I wonder what he's aiming at. A rabbit? A turkey?

Whatever it is, now'd be the perfect time for me to win our little game. You see, if I sneak up on Pa without him noticing (which is hard cos Pa's got bat ears) he has to give me a mint humbug. That's the rule. But spoiling his shot for a candy would land me in *big* trouble, so I'll just have to wait.

I count ten breaths, then ten more (ten's as high as I can count), and then that old rifle looses off a *crack* that echoes far away through the trees. Smoke billows, a pair of doves burst from a nearby bush, and I hold in a cry of delight.

'Dang it!' Pa says.

That means he's missed. He stands up with a grunt and stares hard into the trees.

Now! I scamper towards him, fast, low, silent as a shadow. I see red mud caked on his old leather boots, a kite-shaped sweat stain between his shoulders, tufts of grey hair curling out from under his straw hat. I'm *so close* . . . but as I reach out to tug his shirt he whirls round and shouts, 'Got you!'

'Dang it! When d'you see me?'

'When you were about halfway close. Saw something from the corner of my eye and thought to m'self that's either a giant turkey or Phoebe's trying to sneak up on me again.' He winks and makes a great show of unwrapping a humbug and putting it in his mouth. 'Mmm, delicious,' he says. I shrug like I don't care, but between you and me, I hate losing.

'Better luck next time, my girl.'

I look longingly at the rifle. Pa once said, 'Phoebe, a rifle in some men's hands is a weapon, a terrible thing that can take another's life fast as blinking. But for us it's a tool we use to put food on the table.' And he does too. Rabbits, turkeys and quail for Ma to skin or pluck then turn into stews so delicious my mouth's watering just thinking about 'em.

'Can I help you reload?' I ask.

'Tell you what. You talk me through proceedings just like I taught you – with no mistakes, mind – and I'll let you take the shot. How's that?'

I nod eagerly. Shooting's miles better than getting a humbug.

'All right then . . .' Pa picks up the rifle. 'First step?'

'Put the hammer into the half-cock position.'

Balancing the rifle by holding it part ways along the barrel with his left hand, Pa uses his right thumb to pull back the hammer (that's the metal bit near the stock). He moves smoothly, like he's done this a thousand times . . . I think he fought in a war a long time ago so I s'pose he got lots of practice then.

'Why half-cocked?' he asks.

'Stops the rifle going off by accident.'

'Good. What's next?'

'Open the frizzen and add powder to the pan.'

Pa pushes forward an L-shaped lever (that's the 'frizzen')

then takes a paper tube (the 'cartridge') from his satchel. He bites off the top and carefully pours a thimble's worth of gunpowder into the rounded dish set below the frizzen.

'Close the frizzen, then put the rest of the powder down the barrel.'

Pa snaps the frizzen back into place, then turns the rifle so the barrel's pointing up. There's a trickle as he pours in the rest of the powder.

'Position the wad and ball.'

Pa rests a tiny square of cloth and a lead ball on the end of the barrel then presses them down with his thumb.

'Ram them into the breach.'

Pa pulls a thin steel rod from under the rifle barrel, twirls it round between his fingers, fits it into the barrel's mouth, plunges it down once, twice, three times, then yanks it out.

'Primed and ready to fire,' he says. 'Good girl. Now, come on over to the tree trunk.' I kneel and Pa sets the rifle down beside me. 'Right, now tuck the stock nice and tight into your shoulder. It'll kick some, so be ready. Ma won't be happy if I bring you back all bruised and out of joint. That's it . . . Now, sight down the barrel.'

'So's I can see where the bullet's gonna go.'

'Yep. But remember that little lead ball will start to drop the further away it gets—'

'So if my target's far away, I need to aim high.'

'That's my girl.' Pa's knees crack as he squats next to me.

7

'Take a moment with the rifle. Get a feel for the weight and how it's balanced. In time it'll feel like it's part of you, like another limb.'

Keeping the rifle rested on the tree trunk (I ain't strong enough to hold it up yet, but I will be one day), I trail my fingers over the sharp flint fastened in the hammer, the smooth, gunpowder-dusted frizzen, and the U-shaped spring underneath.

'Comfortable?' Pa asks.

'Mm-mmm.'

'Then make ready to fire.'

I pull the hammer back with my thumb, loving the way it clicks into place.

'Dandy. Now. See that maple yonder, with the branch shaped like a plough handle sticking out? I want you to shoot it clean off.'

I look up at him, a bit disappointed. 'Can't I shoot something for the pot?'

'Naw, you ain't practised enough. Remember, you must always try to kill an animal in one shot so it don't feel any pain. You might miss the vitals and only wound it, and there's no worse sight than a rabbit flopping about with a broken spine.'

I shudder. The branch will do for today, I guess. I curl my finger around the trigger, press my cheek into the stock and peer down that long barrel.

'Line her up,' Pa says, 'and fire when ready.'

The branch is a bit to my left, so I shift position, letting the rifle move with me until it's on target. Then I let out a breath and squeeze the trigger. Heat licks my face as the flint strikes a spark from the frizzen and sets off the gunpowder in the pan. The rifle bucks into my shoulder, but I keep my eyes fixed on the branch.

It shatters halfway along and tumbles to the ground, just as I knew it would.

2

Pa lets me carry his rifle part of the way home. It's heavy and nearly twice as tall as me, so the only way I can manage is by leaning it against my shoulder and holding it steady with both hands.

'A good way to get to know your rifle is to carry it everywhere,' Pa says as we emerge onto the sunlit field, 'but you'd best give it back before your ma sees. You know how she gets.'

'I wish she wouldn't make such a fuss,' I sigh. 'It ain't even loaded.'

'Well, she worries,' Pa replies, tucking the rifle under his arm, 'and that's because she cares about you.'

'But she never scolds Mary Jane or Lydia or the others as much as me.'

Pa laughs. 'That's because your sisters help Ma with the laundry, the cooking and the canning like they're supposed to.'

'But I hate doing that stuff.'

'I know. You're different to your sisters, for sure. I wonder why that is.'

I shrug.

'You're certainly a better shot than I was at your age,' he continues, 'and that's a God-given gift we mustn't waste.'

'But Ma told me off yesterday for just *looking* at the rifle.'

'That's because you were supposed to be cleaning the windows. You listen to your ma and do as she says. All right?'

'All right.'

'Good girl. And when you finish your chores we can go tracking and shooting in the woods to our hearts' content.'

'That's a deal,' I say, feeling more cheerful. 'That branch sure did explode, didn't it?'

'Sure did.' He gives me a humbug. 'But rabbits and quail won't stay still like that branch, so you'll need to practise on moving targets.'

We walk slowly down the track between our two biggest fields. Our farm sits in a dip in the land, and it's all surrounded by trees. Now the wheat's cut I can see right to the horizon. Ohio – that's where we live – is pretty darn flat s'far as I can tell, and it's mostly covered in woodland.

Huh . . . That's probably why they called Woodland Woodland . . . Woodland's the nearest town, although it's still a fair ways away.

'How about you throw sticks in the air for me to shoot?' I suggest.

'But you might hit me,' Pa laughs.

'I sure wouldn't! But you could stand behind a tree if you wanted.'

He thinks on that for a spell. 'Could work. We'll give it a try, anyway.'

'Tomorrow?'

'S'long as you do your chores.'

We reach the bottom of the slope where the fields end and the hard-packed, tree-scattered yard begins. Our cabin sits right in the middle. Ma and Pa built it before I was born. It's got a porch, two chimneys (one for the kitchen stove, one for the fire), three windows and one door.

Then there's the stable where Maple lives, Pa's shed with his workbench and tools all hanging neat and tidy, the water pump that sounds like a donkey's bray when you heave the lever, and way over on the other side of the yard so the ripeness don't reach the cabin, is the latrine.

Lydia, my second-to-eldest (and most annoying) sister, is sitting on a bench on the porch darning a stocking. Her freckled face lights up when she sees me. 'Ooh, Annie, where've you *been*? You're in *such* trouble. You were supposed to milk Pink because Ma wanted to make butter. She's been thundering about all morning making *terrible* threats.'

My heart sinks into my stomach. I'd clean forgot. Or maybe I'd just decided to do it later and gone to the woods to find Pa instead. Either way, Pink's un-milked and Ma's unhappy. Again.

'What's she been sayin'?'

'Well,' Lydia enthuses, 'she said she's going to lock you in the cellar with the rats for the *whole winter*.'

I frown. 'We don't have a cellar.'

'I *know*. Ma's going to make you dig it first.'

Pa taps Lydia's hat so the brim drops over her eyes. 'Don't tease your sister. Is the wagon out? I need to load it up for my trip to the mill.'

'Not yet. Mary Jane's doing it once she's finished in the kitchen,' Lydia says, pushing her hat back up onto her curly brown hair.

'I'd better get on then. I want to be back before night falls.'

I figure I'll turn Ma's thunderstorm to a squall if I milk Pink before she sees me. 'Lydia,' I hiss. 'Where is she?'

'Indoors.' She gives me a wicked grin. 'Shall I call her for you?'

'No! And if she asks, tell her you ain't seen me.'

Lydia shakes her head. 'I cannot lie,' she says primly, and goes back to her darning.

Wondering what I've done to deserve a sister who's such a pill, I creep up to the cabin door (which, luckily, is closed), pick up the pail and head across the yard towards Pink's pasture. But before I make it to the gate, I hear the cabin door open and a voice snap, 'Phoebe Anne Mosey!'

3

Before I go on, I should probably explain that I live in Darke County, Ohio, and my full name is Phoebe Anne Mosey. My four older sisters – that's Mary Jane, Lydia, Liz and Sarah Ellen – and younger brother John, always call me Annie. My other sister, Hulda, is just a baby so she don't call me anything yet. Ma and Pa call me Phoebe or, when they're angry, Phoebe Anne Mosey.

'Phoebe Anne Mosey!'

Darn it. I turn, shoulders slumped, and see Ma on the porch, hands on hips and mad as a hornet. Lydia looks delighted.

'Hold it right there, young lady,' Ma says. 'Where've you been?' But she doesn't even let me reply. 'Never mind. I can guess. You've been beating the Devil round the stump in the woods again, haven't you?'

I nod, confounded as to why Ma always asks me questions she already knows the answer to.

'You were supposed to milk the cow,' she goes on, bristling from top to toe.

Ignoring Lydia's silent laughter, I lift the pail and say, 'I was just about to—'

'Look at the state of you!' Ma marches towards me. 'You've got leaves in your hair, your dress is all grubby. Lord above, I thought I only had one boy.'

'Sorry, Ma . . .'

'And what on earth have you done with your boots?'

I look down at my bare, mud-caked feet. *Dang it!* 'I, er, left 'em on a tree stump.'

'A tree stump?' Ma draws herself up to her full height and points to the pail, then the distant woods, and then at the ground. 'Milk the cow. Fetch your boots. *Wash your feet.* Then come back here, by which time I'll have decided what to do with you.'

'Yes, Ma,' I mumble.

She's already striding back towards the cabin, wide skirt swishing and back straight as a spade handle, when Pa appears from the barn, whistling through his teeth. Ma swerves towards him. They stand close, and after a moment her stiffness just . . . melts away. Pa whispers something into her ear. She laughs and they stroll away up the lane, heads bent towards each other, Pa with his hand resting on the back of Ma's narrow waist.

I trudge into the pasture, wondering what punishment I've let myself in for *this* time. Pink, our beloved brown-and-white Hereford, ambles over when she sees me. 'Morning,' I say as she licks my hand (Pa says she likes the salt). 'I'm in hot water again.' I set the pail in place, grab two teats and start squeezing.

Pink stands patiently while I work, flicking her ears and tail and looking round at me every now and again to see how I'm doing. I stop when the pail's half full, give Pink a thank-you pat and head back to the cabin.

Mary Jane's at the kitchen table brushing beaten egg onto a pie. She's tall with sky-blue eyes and looks just like Ma, 'cept with softer edges and no grey hair. I set the pail down and cover it with a muslin cloth. 'You've got flour on your cheek,' I say.

'Better than having mud on my feet.' Mary Jane picks up a broom and brandishes it at me. 'Outside, Annie – *right* now.'

I retreat to the porch. 'Where's Liz and Sarah?'

'Picking apples. I'm going to bake them for supper tonight.' She pauses. 'The apples, not your sisters.' Mary Jane leans against the door frame, folds her arms and turns her face to the sun. 'Would you like to know a secret about Ma?'

'Is it about her mysterious childhood?' Lydia says from the porch. 'Was she born out of wedlock, left on the riverbank and brought up by gamblers on a Mississippi steamboat?'

Mary Jane ignores her. 'The best way to make her happy is to do what she asks of you. And if you want to make her *really* happy – and maybe avoid the spanking that's coming to you – do something nice that she isn't expecting.'

'What sort of thing?'

Mary Jane bends down and kisses the top of my head. 'That, dear Annie, you'll have to work out on your own.'

I think for a moment. Boots first, so I run back to the woods. After picking them up I head to the stream for a wash. As the water cools my feet, I spy some berry-covered holly bushes. They'll brighten up the cabin and maybe Ma's mood as well, so I cut off some branches with my pocketknife, put on my boots and, being careful not to prick myself on the leaves, head home.

I'm halfway down the track when I see Mary Jane outside the barn harnessing Maple, our chestnut pony with three white feet, to the wagon. Pa, shirt sleeves buttoned at his elbows, is loading the last of the grain sacks. John's on the porch, staring at the ground and looking like the saddest little four-year-old in the world. I guess he's been told he can't go with Pa to the Mill and watch the grain being turned into flour.

Pa kneels in front of him, says a few words then clambers onto the wagon. I wave, but he doesn't see me. Disappointed, I watch as he jerks the reins and clatters down the road; by the time I get to the cabin, he's gone.

Ma's out and about somewhere, so Mary Jane and I hang the holly from the rafters so it'll be a surprise when she gets back. I do my chores for the rest of the afternoon: collecting eggs from the henhouse, filling pails from the water pump, and helping Lydia bathe baby Hulda in a tin bath.

'Why don't you and John take Huldie for a walk while Lydia and I finish getting supper ready?' Mary Jane says as she slides the pie into the oven. 'And chivvy your sisters along – they've been gone for hours and I only sent them out for apples.'

Lydia passes a gurgling Hulda to me. 'Don't drop her,' she says sweetly, 'or leave her on a tree stump.'

I ignore her and head outside. John traipses behind me, still looking sorrowful. We cross the yard and head down the lane that leads to the apple trees. It's getting cold and there's a pile of grey clouds on the horizon.

'Cheer up, John,' I say. 'Pa'll be back soon.'

'I wanted to see the windmill. Watch the sails go round.'

'Well, Pa was in an awful hurry and he works faster on his own,' I say. 'How 'bout we have a race? First one to the orchard can be president for the day.'

John looks at me with solemn eyes. 'But that'll bump Hulda. Let's just walk and be sad.'

'Oh, all right. We'll do that instead.'

I wave when I see Liz and Sarah Ellen strolling up the lane towards us, each carrying an apple-filled basket. 'Mary Jane's sent us to find you,' I say. 'She wants to know why you've taken so long.'

'It's because we've been choosy,' Liz says.

'We only select the best apples for the Moseys' table,' Sarah Ellen adds.

'If a job's worth doing . . .'

'. . . it's worth doing well.'

Liz and Sarah Ellen are always together. Ma reckons they're just like twins.

Wind's really gotten up by the time we get back. It pulls at our hair and swirls up dust devils in the yard. I'm relieved to close the door and breathe in the golden smell of hot pastry.

Ma and Pa built this cabin. Downstairs is one big room. It's got fur rugs on the floor, and walls decorated with a clock that Pa winds every evening, a few pictures of mountains and prairies, and an oval mirror Lydia likes to admire herself in.

There's a big black stove that's always warm, a sideboard with a sink, plates piled on shelves and pots dangling from hooks. There's an open hearth too, with logs piled on either side. Narrow stairs lead up to two bedrooms, one for Ma, Pa and Huldie, and one for Mary Jane cos she's the eldest.

'Getting cold out there,' Liz says as she plonks her basket on the table. 'Oh, that holly livens the place up!'

'That was Annie's idea,' Mary Jane says from the rocking chair.

'She's hoping it'll save her from Ma,' Lydia adds. 'I'm betting it won't work.'

I ignore her and straighten one of my holly sprigs. 'Where is Ma, anyway?'

'She's taken some bread and cottage cheese to Mrs Marshall,' Mary Jane says. 'She'll be back soon. And in the meantime there's still plenty to do around here.'

The cabin's soon a whirl of activity. Hulda's laid down in her crib for a nap. Apples are washed, cored and filled with sugar. The pie is taken from the oven and left to cool on the sideboard. Mattresses are flumphed up, the fire and lanterns are lit, water boiled, vegetables chopped, and plates and cutlery laid for supper.

We've just about finished when the door opens and a red-cheeked Ma bustles in, followed by a gust of wind. 'Storm's coming in. Is everyone here?' She looks relieved when she sees we're all safe and sound.

'Sit down and I'll heat you up some milk,' Mary Jane says, taking Ma's hat.

'Pa's not home,' John says.

'No, dear,' Ma replies with a tired smile. 'He'll be a while yet. We're to have supper without him.'

'But we'll save some for him, won't we?' John's face is deadly serious.

'If we don't, I daresay Pa'll eat *you* up instead,' Lydia says, and she picks him up in a rush and tumbles him onto the bunk bed that we children share at the far end of the cabin.

Ma takes the mug from Mary Jane and settles down in her favourite chair. 'Well,' she says, looking up at my holly, 'that's brightened the place up.'

'Annie picked it from the forest,' Mary Jane says over Lydia and John's laughter. 'It was her idea.'

'Was it now?' Ma says.

'I thought it'd be a nice surprise.' I watch Ma's reaction, but I can't tell if I'm forgiven or not.

'Did you milk Pink?'

'Yes, you're drinking it. And I got the water and helped with Huldie and lots of other chores.'

'As you should. Everyone works in this family.'

'I know that,' I say, feeling my face go hot. 'I'm not lazy.'

'That's true,' Ma says. 'But you put your energies into the wrong things. Laying traps and tracking animals – that's your father's domain. John's too, when he's old enough. But they're not the sort of things a girl should be concerning herself with.'

I open my mouth to protest – I can't help it – but Mary Jane's shaking her head at me. This is a fight for another day, she's saying, and because my oldest sister is one of the wisest people I know, I push my frustration away and say, 'Yes, Ma.'

Perhaps I can get Pa to talk to her . . . make her understand.

Ma beckons me close and gathers me onto her lap. 'All I want is for you to grow up to be a respectable young woman,' she says. I lay my head against her chest as she rocks us back and forth on the chair.

This sure feels nicer than being shouted at in the yard.

4

After the supper things have been washed, we sit together and listen to Ma read a story from the Bible. John picked the one with the loaves and fishes because he loves to hear about food. Then, after saying our prayers, we youngest are sent to bed.

I lay under the blankets, listening as the storm bays at the door, rattles the windows and howls down the chimney like a starving wolf. Icy draughts sneak inside to worry the lanterns and make the herb bundles dangling from the rafters twist and sway.

John's a warm and sleeping lump next to me, but I know Liz and Sarah Ellen are awake in the top bunk because the bed frame creaks every time they fidget. I guess they're thinking the same as me: *Where's Pa?*

Ma, Mary Jane and Lydia sit quietly by the fire. Usually, they'd have gone to bed hours ago. Ma's knitting lays untouched on her lap and she keeps glancing at the cabin door. Mary Jane and Lydia exchange a glance when the wall clock begins to strike.

'Midnight,' Mary Jane murmurs. 'Pa should've been home long ago.'

'The storm must've slowed him down,' Lydia replies. 'Just listen to that wind.'

Ma goes to the window and peeks through the curtains, but there's nothing out there except darkness and swirling snow.

A picture from this afternoon comes into my mind. It's warm and sunny and Pa's clambering onto the wagon with his shirt sleeves rolled up to his elbows. My insides cramp up. I swing my legs out of bed and pad over to my sisters.

'Annie?' Lydia says. 'What are you doing out of bed?'

'You look like you've seen a ghost,' Mary Jane says, taking my hand. 'Whatever's the matter, dear?'

My throat feels tight as I whisper, 'Pa's only got his shirt to keep him warm.'

Mary Jane frowns for a moment, then her eyes grow wide as saucers. 'I think she's right. I remember . . . just a shirt.'

Lydia rushes to the wardrobe. For a moment she just stands there, then she reaches in and brings out Pa's winter coat and scarf. 'He'll be *freezing* out there . . .'

I race for the cabin door, bare feet slapping on the floorboards, but Ma grabs me before I get there. 'Where d'you think you're going?'

'I'm going to find Pa,' I say, squirming to get free. 'He's all alone and lost in the snow—'

'Don't be so foolish, Phoebe,' Ma says, holding me tighter.

'I'll go.' She turns to Lydia. 'Fetch my coat. I'll need a lantern too.'

'I'm coming with you . . .' Hot tears roll down my face and I realise I'm crying.

'No, I said! I need you to stay here and look after John and Hulda.'

Before I can reply, Mary Jane rushes to the window. 'It's Pa! He's back!'

Sweet relief wells up inside me. I clasp my hands and send a grateful prayer to heaven.

'Oh, thank God!' Ma throws open the cabin door. Wind howls in, snuffing lanterns and swallowing the warmth in a single gulp. There's two thumps as Liz and Sarah Ellen jump down from their bunk. 'What's happening?' John says sleepily.

Ma thrusts herself through the door with her arm raised against the storm. 'Jacob? Are you well?' The wind snatches her words and throws them far away.

Mary Jane and Lydia follow, lanterns swinging. Shadows leap and lurch in a world turned white. The wagon's stopped in the yard. Maple's facing the cabin door, head down and shivering. Snow's piled on her back, and her whiskers and eyelashes are stiff with ice.

My relief shrivels and dies. There's something wrong with Pa. He's slumped forward so I can't see his face, and he's not moving or speaking even though we're calling his name.

Mary Jane and Lydia hold their flickering lanterns up as Ma takes his shoulders and gives him a shake. He barely moves. His limbs are rigid. Like he's frozen solid. Ma gives a cry that I hardly hear over the wind.

I climb up the other side of the wagon. Ma's working at his hands, trying to unclasp them from the reins. His fingertips are black, like they've been dipped in ink. I try unbending one, but it won't budge even a tiny bit; I'm frightened if I pull too hard it'll snap clean off.

As Lydia, Liz and Sarah Ellen unhitch Maple and lead her to the barn, Ma and I fiddle, tug and unwind the reins from between Pa's poor fingers. It seems to take forever, and Ma and I are weeping by the time we've got them free.

Mary Jane lifts me down from the wagon and hands me the lantern. 'Hold this while I get him inside,' she yells over the shrieking wind. Together they lift Pa to the ground and half-walk, half-drag him indoors. I follow and close the door on the storm.

Ma and Mary Jane lay Pa by the hearth. He's still in the same position as on the wagon – legs drawn up, arms bent at the elbows. I feel the cold coming off him, and the only reason I know he's not dead is because he's making a horrible *rurr-rurr-rurr* sound from behind teeth bit hard together.

'What shall I do?' I whisper.

'Bank up the fire,' Mary Jane replies. 'We need to heat the whole place up.'

I throw on some logs and stir the embers with a poker until it crackles to life. A wide-eyed John tugs my arm. 'What's wrong with Pa?'

'He got caught in the storm,' Mary Jane says, pulling blankets from the chest by the window. 'But we're warming him up as fast as we can.'

'Phoebe,' Ma says, 'help me get his boots off.'

We work together to yank the stiff leather boots from his legs. Next, we peel off his socks. His feet are like ice blocks. Ma lifts them onto her lap and starts to rub them.

'Jacob, Jacob, Jacob,' she sobs. 'Please just *say* something.'

John starts to cry as Mary Jane strips Pa out of his soaking shirt. She places her ear against his chest and listens. 'His heart's beating, but it's weak.' I help her wrap him up with blankets until only his face can be seen. His eyes are moving all over the place but they don't seem to be looking at anything.

The fire's roaring and the cabin's warming up when the door opens and Lydia, Liz and Sarah Ellen tumble inside.

'Maple's safe and sound,' Lydia says through chattering teeth. 'She's tuckered out but I think she'll be all right. Heaven knows how she found her way home in this.'

'How's Pa?' Liz asks, brushing snow from her shoulders.

'Has he said anything?' Sarah Ellen adds.

'No,' Mary Jane replies. 'He's frozen stiff.'

'He must have been in that storm for hours.' Lydia turns

to me and gasps. 'Annie! You're shaking like a leaf, and no wonder! Going outside in just your night things and nothing on your feet.' She ushers me closer to the fire, drags the blanket from my bed and bundles me up.

Liz and Sarah Ellen kneel behind Pa and rub his arms and back. Liz leans close to his ear. 'Pa, can you hear us? We're all with you. You're *home*. Speak to us so we know you're all right.'

'He needs the Doc,' Mary Jane says.

'I know, but we can't fetch him till the storm passes,' Lydia replies. 'We can only pray that it clears up soon, and the roads ain't blocked when it does.'

'Will you go, Mary Jane, when you can?' Ma says. 'I don't want to leave him.'

'Of course.'

So we wait. Ma at Pa's feet, Mary Jane and Lydia by his head, and Liz, Sarah Ellen and John sitting behind. And all the while the storm rages.

5

Liz shakes me from a cold and swirling nightmare.

'Wake up, Annie. We need you.'

I wonder why I'm lying by the fire. Then I remember . . . I crawl from under the blanket, feeling shaky and tearful. Night's passed and so's the storm. Through the window I see footprints and cart tracks in the snow; Mary Jane must've gone to get Doc Barker from Woodland.

Pa's in my bed under lots of blankets. He's shivering and still making that *rurr-rurr-rurr* noise. I force myself to creep closer and see his eyes rolling about under half-closed lids. Ma's standing rigid at the end of the bed. I take her hand. 'Has he said anything?' I ask. She shakes her head.

'And his breathing's still so shallow,' Sarah Ellen sighs.

'When'll Mary Jane be back?' Ma doesn't answer so I give her hand a tug. 'Ma? When's the Doc arriving?'

Ma's brow creases. 'What? Oh, I don't know . . .'

'This afternoon at the earliest, I'd say,' Lydia says as she clatters down the stairs. 'And later if he's on his rounds. It's up to us to look after Pa for the time being. Ah, Annie! Get dressed and make us some breakfast, would you?'

'I couldn't eat a morsel,' Sarah Ellen says.

'Me neither,' I say.

'You'll eat, both of you.' Lydia sounds more like Ma or Mary Jane than her usual self. 'You need to keep your strength up.' She wags a finger at me. 'Go on! Dressed, then breakfast.'

I do as I'm told and am just pulling my boots on when the cabin door opens. For a moment I hope it might be Mary Jane with the Doc, but it's only Liz, bent backwards with a pile of logs in her arms. John puffs in after her, dragging a basket of kindling.

'Right, let's get this fire stoked,' Liz says. She speaks brightly – for John and my sake probably – but I see her worried glance at Pa.

Somehow, Lydia manages to persuade Ma to lie down for a while. In the meantime we tend to Pa, make breakfast and wait impatiently for Mary Jane's return.

The sun's on its way down when the cart rattles into the yard.

'Thank the Lord,' Ma says, throwing the door open and letting Mary Jane and Doc Barker inside.

'Afternoon, Mrs Mosey,' the Doc says. 'Mary Jane's explained all. Has Mr Mosey spoken since his return?'

Ma shakes her head. 'Not a word.'

'Any attempts to communicate? Hand signals? Sounds?'

'No. Nothing.'

'He's over here,' I say, ushering him to the bed. 'Quickly, Doc!'

'Hush now, Phoebe,' Ma hisses. 'The doctor knows his business.'

'It's all right, Mrs Mosey,' Doc Barker says. 'She's right, time is of the essence.'

I stare fascinated at his big old bag. It's made from cracked brown leather and rattles when he sets it down. Surely he's got something in there that will cure Pa? We all stand anxiously around as he sets to work. First, he puts a thin glass tube in Pa's mouth.

'What's that?' I ask.

'A thermometer,' Lydia whispers, 'to take Pa's temperature. Now hush.'

Leaving the thermo-thing in place, Doc lifts an eyelid with his thumb and peers into Pa's eyes. 'Mmmm . . .' Then he examines Pa's blackened fingertips and toes, whips out the thermometer and squints at the reading. Next, he folds down the blankets, places his ear against Pa's chest and listens. We all wait, hardly daring to breathe as he sits back up, puts his bits and pieces away and snaps the bag shut. His face is grave when he looks at Ma.

'Your husband is very ill,' he says. 'The cold's got right into him. Pneumonia. Frostbite. I'm afraid I can't say with any certainty that he'll survive. Being subjected to hours in that freezing storm in nothing but a shirt' – he shakes his head – 'I'm amazed he got here at all.'

Ma grips the bedstead so hard her knuckles go white. 'You mean . . . he might die?'

'You must prepare yourselves for the possibility. He might linger in this state for some time, and then suddenly pass.'

I shake my head in disbelief. Pa's the strongest person I know. He drives the plough for hours in blazing sun and driving rain. He lifts me up and spins me round like I'm no heavier than a feather. I don't believe he'll die, no matter how cold he got.

I take his hand and wait for a sign to say he knows I'm close – a twitching finger, a fluttering eyelid, a muttered word . . . but I have to push my disappointment away when nothing happens.

'Why won't he speak to us?' I ask. 'It's like he doesn't even know we're here.'

'I can't say for certain, young lady,' the doc replies. 'But being exposed to such cold can affect the mind as well as the body.' He raises his finger. 'However, I believe appearances can deceive, and in some deep recess in his mind he knows you're close. My advice is to behave as if he understands every word, gesture and kindness you extend.'

'What else should we do?' Mary Jane asks.

'Keep him warm and clean. Bandage his frostbit fingers and feet, but loosely. Give him as much soup and warm milk as he'll take. Treat him like a newborn and you won't go far wrong.' I take in every word, determined to do all the Doc says. He stands and picks up his bag. 'I'll be back in a couple days to check on him.'

'Thank you,' Ma says in a faraway voice, and he follows Mary Jane outside.

6

It's been two weeks and Pa still hasn't said a word. He moans sometimes and looks aimlessly around the cabin, but mostly he just lies on his back, shivering, sweating and breathing in shallow gasps.

We're following Doc Barker's advice. The fire's always alight, I make darn sure of *that*. Three times a day Mary Jane and Ma prop Pa up against the pillows and spoon-feed him soup followed by warm milk sweetened with sugar. But he just keeps getting thinner.

He's never alone. We take it in turns to sit by him, morning, noon and night. Lydia tells him about the silly jokes she plays on us. Mary Jane reads to him, sometimes from the Bible, sometimes from her favourite book of plants and birds. She even holds the pages up so he can see the pictures. Liz and Sarah Ellen sing hymns with their sweet, clear voices. Ma sits with her head bent close to his, talking quietly. Perhaps she's remembering good times they've had. Perhaps she's praying.

Poor John's afraid of the pale, coughing man in his bed, and only gets close when someone's with him.

I hold Pa's dear hand and, so he knows I've not forgotten, I go over all the things he's taught me on our trips in the woods. Like how to lay corn traps, track rabbits, spot a fox den, make a fire, build a shelter from branches, and load a Kentucky long rifle.

'Remember,' I say, 'you said you'd teach me to hit moving targets. You're going to stand behind a tree and throw sticks in the air.'

I squeeze his hand. Before the tears come, I remember my new rule: never cry in front of Pa. My other rule (made the day the Doc said he might die) is no matter how bad things get, don't give up hope. More weeks pass. Outside, the ground is hard white, the trees soot black and the sky iron grey. Doc Barker comes every week, tells us we're doing the right things and leaves a bill behind. We have a pile now, and Ma frets over them with Mary Jane when she thinks we're asleep.

Pa's the same. He has no voice and no expression. It's like the storm stole his spirit but left the body behind, to sweat and cough and moan and be sick in a pail by the bed. My pa is skin and bone. He makes the whole cabin smell, no matter how often we bathe him and change the bedlinen. At night, the rattle in his chest carries to the bedroom upstairs where I sleep with Ma and John. It keeps me awake. I lie there, staring at the sloping roof beams and think, *How many more breaths does he have, and what will I do if they stop?*

I know I cry in my sleep, because when I wake my pillow is wet.

I've learned that hope is hard to hold onto. Especially when Pa's shivering even though the cabin's hot, or he can't keep his food down, or when I hear Ma sobbing when she reckons there's no one around. On those days I think about how long it's been since I heard Pa's voice, or saw his eyes crinkle into a smile just for me. I wonder if those things will ever happen again.

But on other days, after Pa's had a quiet night and his face is so peaceful it looks like he's just sleeping, hope blooms like a flower. I talk to him as I bounce around doing my chores, certain that one day soon he'll warm up and come back to us.

Every morning at sunrise I get out of bed, wash in the basin on the dresser, pull on my stockings, dress and boots, and creep downstairs so's not to wake anyone. I ask whoever's sitting with Pa how he's been and give him a kiss on the cheek.

Then it's time to face the outdoors. I put on my winter coat, scarf, hat and mittens, open the door just wide enough to squeeze through, and breathe in my first mouthful of winter air.

I fill a basket with logs from the woodpile and drag it across the icy yard. It's hard work, but that's good because it warms me up and takes my mind off things. The water pump froze up weeks ago, so I use a shovel to gather the freshest snow I can find and dump it in a pail to be melted over the stove.

Then it's back inside, into the blessed warm. I pile the logs by the hearth, poke the fire to get it blazing, light the stove and put a pot of coffee on. Next is breakfast: a dollop of porridge from a saucepan, which I cover with milk and sugar. Pa called . . . *calls* it Winter Breakfast.

When everyone's up and about (John's usually last) we all gather around Pa's bed to say a prayer. Ma speaks the words and we listen with our heads bowed and our hands clasped. Milking Pink's next, so back outside I go. In winter she lives in the barn with Maple, out of the wind and feeding on the hay Pa harvested in fall. The barn smells of straw and animals. I love it.

Our cats live here too. They're not pets, but they're not totally wild either. The big black-and-white tom likes to watch me from high up in the rafters. The ginger queen is friendlier and usually comes out from a corner somewhere to say hello with her fur covered in hay. They get rid of rats, and we repay them with scraps.

After milking Pink, I help Lydia make soup and bread, fetch yet *more* wood and *more* snow, take baby Hulda outside for some fresh air (I love how surprised she looks when the cold hits her face) and try to sit still as Mary Jane teaches me and John our numbers and letters on a little blackboard.

It's boring, but she makes us.

*

I'm not sure what time it is but it's still dark outside, the birds aren't awake yet and I'm sitting by Pa holding his hand. His face looks soft in the lantern light and he's resting easy. His chest rises and falls under the covers and little whistles of air come from his nose.

'I know it'd normally be Mary Jane sitting with you at this hour,' I say, 'but she's not feeling well so I'm here instead. She said to say how sorry she is, and she'll make up for it when she's better.' I watch for a response, but he just breathes and whistles, breathes and whistles . . .

The cabin's warm and my eyes are getting heavy. I shake my head to stop myself falling asleep, then gasp as Pa's fingers tighten around mine, hold them fast for one . . . two . . . *three whole seconds!* I watch his face, praying he'll open his eyes . . . My excitement dies when Pa doesn't stir another muscle. But I won't give up hope. No, *sir.*

'S'all right, Pa,' I say, patting his hand. 'I know you'll come back when you're ready. I'll be waiting. We all will.'

It's February, two months after that dreadful storm, and I'm walking down the lane from the woods with a bundle of kindling under my arm. I stop dead as a scream tears through the cabin walls and startles a mourning dove from its perch on the roof.

The front door bangs open and Ma bursts out, bent double as if she's about to be sick. She staggers across the yard, clawing at her hair and face, before collapsing into the snow. Mary Jane and Lydia are with her in a moment, kneeling one on either side with their arms wrapped around her shoulders. Ma's scream becomes a howl as raw as the winter air.

The hope I've nurtured for so long shatters. Pa's gone and nothing will be the same again.

I can't bear to go back to the cabin and see his lifeless body, or hear Ma's cries, or see my sisters' heartbroken faces, so I drop the kindling and run back up the track. I plunge into the woods, our special place, and I don't stop until I reach the oak where I practised my shooting the last time me and Pa were together. The last time. The last time *ever*.

I collapse by the trunk and let the cold fill me. Everything blurs as the tears come, and there's a block of ice in my chest that I know will never melt.

7

SPRING 1866

It's early morning. Dew-covered cobwebs sparkle in the sun and I'm heading to the woods to see if any birds have fallen into my corn traps. If they have, we'll eat meat tonight. If not, we'll have to make do with turnip soup thickened with pearl barley again; I'm trying not to get my hopes up because I've only snared a few birds so far.

We buried Pa a month ago at Mendenhall Cemetery. The funeral cost most of our savings, which adds more worry to the pile. His grave marker reads 'Jacob Mosey, Died Feb 11th 1866 Aged 65' but misses out all the important things, like his smile, his warmth and how he cared for us all.

After Pa died, I decided pretty darn quick I was going to use the outdoor skills he taught me to help the family. It's what he would have wanted. 'Ground birds like turkeys and quail make paths, just like people do,' Pa told me. 'Keep an eye out for trails of beaten down undergrowth, stray feathers and droppings. They'll be the best places to lay a trap.'

So, one morning, I grabbed a shovel and found a turkey

path in the woods. A few minutes of hacking at frozen ground told me I needed a better plan, so I melted the ground with a brush fire and managed to scrape a few inches off the surface. Then I made another fire, dug a bit further down, and so on. It took *days*, and I don't know how many times I screamed with frustration when the fire refused to light.

Once the hole was deep enough, I covered it with straw and left a trail of grain leading up to the edge. The notion is that a ground bird will peck at the grain, fall through the straw and not be able to get out. I've scraped four traps now, and I've never been prouder of anything else that I've done in my life. I think Pa would be proud too.

The sack of straw bumps against my back as I hop over the stream to check my first trap. It's empty; even the grain trail's still here. The next trap's another bust. So's the next. 'Are you getting wise to me?' I mutter as I scatter more grain around my last and disappointingly empty hole. 'Or is this just an unlucky day?'

I sit on a tree stump and prop my chin on my hands. I hate going home empty handed – makes me feel ashamed. I hear animals rustling in the undergrowth and even catch a glimpse of turkeys. If only I could use Pa's rifle . . .

My family's struggling. We're having to do all the heavy jobs Pa used to do like chop wood and clear stones from the fields. Last week I had to clamber onto the roof with Mary Jane to fix a leak.

Ma's got work helping the locals, looking after babies, the old and sick, cooking, cleaning and doing laundry. It means she's away all day and exhausted when she gets home. And yet, every night without fail, she gathers us all by the fire and washes our hands and feet in a basin, brushes our hair, takes John and Huldie onto her lap and sings hymns and prays to God to watch over us.

It's getting dark so I'd better head home. I just hope I'll have better luck with my traps tomorrow.

John and I are back in our bed, but only after Ma changed the mattress cover and stuffed it with clean straw. I'm thankful, but it still feels strange to sleep where Pa died. It's dark at this end of the cabin. John's curled up beside me and there's no movement above so I know Liz and Sarah Ellen are asleep too. But I'm wide awake and listening to Ma, Mary Jane and Lydia talk in low voices around the kitchen table.

'I don't know what to do, girls,' Ma says. 'We've no savings left. I'm working every hour God sends, but the dollar and a bit I earn each week isn't enough even to keep the pantry stocked, let alone pay the mortgage on this place.'

'And we still owe Doc Barker,' Mary Jane says, shuffling

the bills around on the table. 'He's been patient, but he won't wait forever.'

'He can wait till Judgement Day s'far as I'm concerned,' Lydia snaps. 'He didn't help Pa one bit.'

'Hush,' Mary Jane chides. 'Cold took Pa, not the Doc.'

'Well, he needs paying, and quickly,' Ma says. 'I'll not have people saying the Moseys don't make good on their debts. We'll have to scare up the money from somewhere.'

'I checked our stores today and I reckon we've enough corn to seed the top fields, but we'll need to buy extra if we want a full harvest.'

'More expense?' Lydia says.

'Afraid so.' Mary Jane covers a cough with her hand and takes a sip of milk.

'Can we even hope to do all that work without Pa?' Lydia asks. 'The ploughing, reaping and threshing? Ma, you can't help because of your nursing duties, and one of us always has to keep an eye on Huldie . . .'

Ma puts her hands over Lydia's and Mary Jane's. Her voice is fierce. 'I know we've got a hard row to hoe, but if anyone can do it, my girls can. If it weren't for you, I don't know what I'd do. And I'll tell you something else, I thank the Lord for our Phoebe and her clever traps.'

'Yes, she's quite the woodsman,' Lydia says. 'Or woodswoman, I should say!'

'Pa taught her well,' Mary Jane adds.

'And to think that dear man actually thought we didn't know what they were up to when they trotted up to the woods all those times,' Ma says with a sad smile.

'He thought you didn't approve,' Lydia says.

'I didn't. I *still* don't. But needs must when the Devil drives.'

The pride I feel fades when I remember my empty traps.

8

FALL 1866

There's no one home when I get back and flop down at the kitchen table; I believe Ma's swallowed her pride and has trekked off to Woodland to get a few dollars for her best dress. My legs are tired from another hopeless trek checking my traps. All empty. *Again*. It's been days since I brought any game back, and I feel wretched.

Wretched and hungry. *So* hungry.

It's a gnawing, empty feeling, impossible to ignore. Makes me shaky and muzzy-headed. Snappy too. Yesterday I yelled at John for dropping a jar of pickled radishes. He was so shocked because I *never* shout.

There's a bowl of apples on the table. Most are half-rotten and wrinkly. It'll be my job to cut out the worst of the brown bits and hope there's enough left to make a pie. But we've no sugar or currants to add to the mix, so it won't be anywhere near as nice as the ones we used to make.

Through the window I see Lydia and a pale Mary Jane lead Maple from the barn. They're off for another day's hard work in the fields. When they plod back at sunset they're so tired they can hardly stand. I glimpsed Marv Jane getting changed the other morning and she's gotten so thin I could see her ribs.

I clench my hands into fists. My traps aren't enough.

I swivel around on the chair and gaze up at Pa's rifle gathering dust over the hearth. 'A rifle is a tool we use to put food on the table,' he'd said, but Ma's forbidden me from touching it, let alone firing it. It's senseless and maddening and I simply can't *stand* it any more.

I drag the chair over, climb up, stand on my tiptoes and, using both upstretched hands, lift the rifle down from its hooks. A quick rummage in the chest by the window unearths the powder and shot bag. I check inside and find the gunpowder horn and a dozen cartridges already prepared (by Pa, I think, and my breath hitches). I sling it over my shoulder and shorten the strap so it hangs comfortably by my hip.

With the rifle balanced against my shoulder, I peek through the window to make sure no one's around and head on up to the woods. I don't stop until I reach our fallen oak; if Pa reckoned it was a good place to bag a bird, that's good enough for me.

First things first: load the rifle. I know the steps and I've watched Pa do it many times, but I've never done it myself. Thing is, there's a lot that can go wrong. Use too little gunpowder and the rifle won't fire. Use too much and the barrel might explode and I'll lose an eye and half my face.

All right, Annie. You just need to be careful.

The rifle's taller than me (I'm quite short for my age – something Lydia teases me about), which makes it impossible to load when it's standing upright. I rest it at an angle on the tree trunk and get to work. It takes a few minutes to pour the gunpowder, ram home the bullet and prime the pan. Then I hurry down to the clearing, spread some grain on the ground, head back, take up my firing position and slide the rifle forward so it's resting on the trunk.

And now comes the part that Pa said was the hardest. The wait.

Now, I don't like sitting still. I like to run around, climb trees and explore. Before Pa died, when we youngest children were not always needed on the farm, Ma sometimes sent us to the school in Woodland to learn letters and numbers and adding and subtracting and (worst of all) multiplication. I *hated* it. I fidgeted, swung my feet and once got the teacher so mad she threw a chalk at me. I couldn't wait for the bell to ring so I could go outside again.

Yet here I am, having to be quieter and stiller than in the classroom. And the tree trunk is cold and wet and not very comfortable to lean on (I'll bring a blanket next time). And I might be here for hours and not see hide nor hair of a rabbit or a squirrel or a quail. And even if they do make an appearance I might miss the shot, and if I've loaded the rifle wrong it might blow up in my hands. And

I know for *sure* Ma's going to be furious with me for going hunting.

But I don't mind any of that. Not one bit. I'm doing what Pa would have done for us if he was here, and that makes me feel closer to him.

Fingers of sunlight poke through the trees and feel along the forest floor. I hear life all around: birdcalls and wing-flutters from the branches above, squirrels scampering up trees behind, twigs snapping and bracken rustling in the distance. But nothing in my clearing. Not yet . . .

I'm about to stand and stretch my back when I hear a warble, and from out of the undergrowth struts a wild turkey. Pa said I must have real sharp eyesight when I described an eastern bluebird perched so far away he couldn't even see it, but I don't need good eyesight to see this grand specimen! His dark feathers are all puffed up and his tail's splayed out like a rich lady's fan. He spies the grain and starts to peck.

Very slowly, I tuck the stock into my shoulder and pull back the hammer – *snick* – with my right hand. I hold the barrel gently with my left, but keep the rifle resting on the tree trunk so it stays steady.

My heart thumps as I line up the rifle. It would be easier to hit the turkey's plump body, but that might not kill it straightaway. I must hit the head or neck. Harder shots, and if I miss he'll be long gone before I can reload.

The problem is the turkey's never still! It pecks away, looks up for a heartbeat, then it's back to pecking again. I aim the rifle so it's pointing just above the turkey's bald and bobbing head, then I give a whistle. The turkey looks up, alerted but not frightened by the noise, and stands quite still. I adjust my aim and pull the trigger.

9

It's a really big turkey!

At first I didn't know how I was to carry it and the rifle at the same time. But by slinging the turkey over one shoulder and balancing the rifle against the other, I'm getting used to their different weights and how they move, and am managing to walk home at my usual brisk pace.

Through the cabin window I hear Ma and Mary Jane talking, and I think that's Liz singing *Skip To My Lou*. I lean the rifle against the wall and march inside with the turkey. All talk and singing stops when they see me and my prize.

Liz gives a cry of delight and claps her hands. 'Oh, Annie, look what you've brought us!'

'My stars, what a bounty!' Mary Jane beams. She opens the back window and calls, 'Lydia, Sarah Ellen, John, come here and see what your clever sister's done!'

My sisters and little John surround me, chattering excitedly as I place the turkey on the table.

'This will last us for days . . . !'

'We can roast it, then make soup from the leftovers . . .'

'Aren't those feathers beautiful? I shall make something from them . . .'

Ma stands by the sink, drying her hands on a cloth. She watches me, and I can tell that she's doing that strange grown-up thing of being happy and unhappy at the same time.

'You must have dug a really big trap for this one,' Sarah Ellen says.

Oh well, here goes . . .

'Not this time,' I say, and I get Pa's rifle from outdoors and lean it against the table.

The room goes quiet. Mary Jane, Lydia, Liz, Sarah Ellen and John all turn to look at the two empty hooks over the fireplace, then stare back at me. Mary Jane gives me one of her gentle smiles then casts a sidelong glance at Ma. Lydia's grinning and shaking her head. Liz and Sarah Ellen's mouths are little 'o's of amazement.

'You shot it?' John squeaks.

'Yep. Right through the head. A clean kill.'

This should be a happy moment, 'cept for the fact that Ma's gaze hasn't left me since the moment I brought the turkey in. Her mouth's become a hard, lipless line turned down at the edges.

'Everybody out,' she says in a low voice I've come to dread. 'I want to speak to Phoebe.'

'Ma—' Mary Jane begins.

'Outside, right now!'

My sisters and a confused-looking John file out. Lydia gives my hand a squeeze as she slips by and closes the door . . . leaving me alone with Ma, who's turned into a black tower of wrath. Her neck's rashed-up pink and her face is *quivering*. We look at each other over the turkey lying between us on the table.

'You took your father's rifle,' she says.

'I wanted to—'

Dishes rattle as she slams both palms onto the table. 'How *dare* you? I've told you time and time again not to touch that wretched thing. I made you promise that you wouldn't, and you've broken your word. How can I trust you now? How can I leave you alone and not be worrying myself sick that you're just going to do any damn thing you please? Don't you think I've enough to cope with?' She leans over the table and screams, '*Don't you?*'

I step back on shaking legs. My stomach's flip-flopping around like a spine-shot rabbit and there's a strange fluttering sensation down the side of my face. I've seen Ma angry lots of times, but never like this.

'My traps were empty again and I wanted to—'

'You broke your promise and you took something that doesn't belong to you. That's your father's rifle, not yours. You waited, then you sneaked out without anyone knowing because you knew what you were doing was wrong.'

Broke. Took. Sneaked. Wrong. The words hit me like stones.

Tears prickle behind my eyes. I want to say sorry so that Ma's anger will disappear ... but I can't, because the apology would be a lie. Instead, I shake my head and say, 'I took the rifle to put food on the table, and I only sneaked out because I knew my sisters would stop me to keep me from getting into trouble with *you.*'

'Yes, you'd have been in trouble. And you're in trouble now.' Ma snatches up the rifle and holds it out as if it was a live rattlesnake. 'This is dangerous, Phoebe. Use it wrong and you could end up hurt, or even killed.'

'I was careful. Pa taught me—'

'Oh, and how I wish I'd nipped all that nonsense in the bud right from the start. Jacob was a good man but taking a little girl hunting wasn't right. Wasn't proper.'

Now it's my turn to feel a flare of anger. What does she mean, *proper?*

'I don't see what's wrong with doing what I'm afly at,' I say, louder than I'd intended.

'That's because you're too young to understand. Shooting and trapping, that's men's business. It's not for women.'

I want to scream so loud that everyone in Darke County can hear. 'But *why*?'

For a split-second Ma looks confounded, then she says, 'That's just the way it is. It's what I was raised to believe, and so was everyone else in civilised parts of the world.' She glares at me. 'It's what I thought I'd raised you to believe too.'

'Pa didn't think that way.'

'He wasn't judged on the way his daughters behaved. As the mother, that's *my* burden to bear, and people will talk and snipe and gossip if they see you traipsing about on your own, grubbing about in rabbit holes like a moonshiner's urchin.'

'Who *cares* what they say?'

'I do! I'm talking about our reputation among our friends and neighbours, and like it or not, what they think about us *matters*. And don't think this is about my vanity, Phoebe. We might need their help one day, and they'll be more willing to lend it if they have a high opinion of us. I might even want to marry again someday, so I must maintain good standing in the community to improve my prospects.'

'Married?' I cry. 'Pa's only just d—' I choke on the word – I just can't say it. 'We've just lost Pa, and you're thinking about getting *married*?'

'I said I'm considering the possibility.' Ma looks stubborn, but there's a pink blush on her cheeks that might be shame. 'I admit that the thought of going alone into old age frightens me. And besides, it'd be as much for you children as it would be for me. We need a man to keep this place running, do the heavy work . . .'

'But you've always said it's up to us to help ourselves. And look, Ma' – I rest my hand on the turkey's soft feathers – 'just look at all this food.'

The clock ticks the seconds away until eventually Ma sags.

She pulls two chairs out from the table. 'Come here.' We sit for a while, both looking at the turkey. Eventually she says, 'This will keep us going for days. Have you seen how thin Mary Jane's getting?'

I nod and shift my chair closer to her. 'I can bring home more,' I say. 'I'm a daisy shot. Pa said so.'

'Oh, Jacob,' Ma whispers. 'He loved all you children, but I think he felt a special bond with you. You're so alike.'

I know Ma's thinking about everything we've said and I've a strong urge to pipe up, but I know if Mary Jane were here, she'd catch my eye and press a finger to her lips. *Patience, Annie. Give Ma some time.* So I wait.

'You can continue to hunt, trap and shoot,' Ma says, 'because it would be foolish to waste a skill that God, in his mysterious wisdom, has given you.' A weight lifts from my shoulders and I want to dance around the room, but Ma's face is still serious. She holds up a finger. 'But there are conditions. One. When you take the rifle you must tell me exactly where you're going.'

I nod.

Two fingers are held up. 'Two. You must take the utmost care when loading and shooting. Never rush or do anything sloppily.'

As if I would! But all I say is, 'Yes.'

Three fingers. 'Three. You will dress properly even when you're tramping around the woods alone. You will wear your boots, a hat, and keep your clothes clean and your hair neat. I want you to be presentable – *respectable* – even with a rifle on your shoulder and rabbits hanging from your belt.'

'Yes, Ma.'

Four fingers. 'And, Phoebe Anne Mosey, you must always come home to me unharmed and in one perfect piece.'

I take her calloused hands and promise I always will.

'Now then,' she says, wiping her eyes, 'what's the betting that your silly sisters are eavesdropping right behind that door? Let them in, because they've got a turkey to pluck.'

10

EARLY SUMMER 1867

'Annie! A-nnie! Where *are* you?'

That's Lydia blundering through the undergrowth somewhere behind me. The ring-neck quail I've been tracking freezes for a moment then scurries off into the undergrowth. I raise my rifle to take a shot but it's too late. It's gone. Dang it!

'I'm over here,' I call, knowing Lydia will never be able to spot me in my dark hunting outfit of a brown knee-length dress, thick woollen stockings, sturdy leather boots, a red-and-white kerchief around my neck, and Pa's powder and shot bag over my shoulder. My favourite part's the straw hat that Mary Jane decorated with feathers from that first turkey I shot. She said, 'Just because an outfit is practical, that doesn't mean it needs to be drab.'

I've gone rifle-hunting several times a week for about a year and I'm much better now. My back, shoulders and arms have got strong enough for me to aim and take a steady shot without leaning the rifle on anything. Ma still don't like it, but she knows that without the game I bring home we'd have starved half to death months ago.

As it happens, through sheer hard work and determination, we Moseys have survived. We brought in the harvest last fall and the money we made – along with Ma's wages – got us through another winter *and* paid off Doc Barker's bills. It's a hard life, but we're getting through it together.

'There you are!' Lydia says, crashing through the undergrowth like a buffalo. 'Any luck?'

'Some,' I say, showing her the brace of quail hanging from my belt.

'Well, bully for you!' She slips her arm through mine. 'Come on, it's nearly suppertime and Ma'll be home soon. You really do lose all track of time when you're up here, don't you?'

We make our way into the early evening sunshine. The fields are green with young wheat.

'I thought I might embroider my dress,' I say.

'Good idea. I've some coloured thread you can borrow.'

'I might need your help. Maybe we can do it tonight?'

'All right,' she says gaily. 'I'll try to fit you in between my social engagements. I've been invited to dine at the White House by the President.'

'How fancy! May I accompany you?'

'Of course! You can present those birds. I'm sure the First Lady would *love* to do some plucking.'

We chatter all the way to the cabin, passing Liz and John brushing Maple down in the yard. The cabin door's open so we skip right on inside. Lydia goes upstairs to fetch her thread while I plonk the birds on the table, stand on a chair to put the rifle back and sit down with a contented sigh.

Mary Jane's peering in the oven at a huge pie that already smells delicious. 'How'd you do today?' she asks.

'Bagged a brace. Would've been three but Lydia scared one off. Does that mean I get her share of the meat?'

'Yes, I think that's done . . .' Mary Jane straightens up, squints at me and says, 'What? No! Of course not. Equal shares, as always.'

'I was only joking.'

'Very funny. There are some scraps outside on a plate. Can you take them to the cats?'

'All right.'

I'm making my way across the yard when I hear a rasping cough coming from the kitchen. Liz and John look over at the door and we all jump at the sound of smashing crockery. I dash back to the cabin, dropping the scraps plate on the way, and stop dead on the threshold. Liz and John run into me and I stumble inside.

'What was that?' Lydia cries as she clatters down the stairs.

Mary Jane lies face-down on the floor. She must have been taking the pie from the oven, fallen and landed on it, because she's surrounded by steaming lumps of meat, shattered pottery and a spreading pool of gravy.

Lydia rushes over and nearly slips in the mess. Fighting

down panic, I kneel next to her and together we roll Mary Jane onto her back. We all gasp. Her lips are slick with blood.

'Mary Jane, can you hear me?' I say in a quivering voice.

Lydia scrapes the roasting bits of pie from Mary Jane's chest, but her arms and neck are already covered in burns.

'What happened?' Liz cries.

'I heard her coughing,' I reply, 'and you know how thin she's gotten. I think she's' – a lump chokes my throat – 'I think she's really sick.'

'I should've made her go see the Doc weeks ago,' Lydia says, sounding disgusted with herself.

'Don't blame yourself,' Liz says. 'You know what Mary Jane's like.'

'I know, but we'd have found the money from *somewhere*...'

'Well, never mind that now,' Liz sighs. 'Let's get her into bed. We'll use yours, Annie, until we can move her upstairs.'

Between us we get Mary Jane undressed and tucked up under the covers; she opens her eyes – oh, the relief! – just as Lydia places a damp cloth on her forehead. 'What happened?' she croaks, looking around at us.

'You fell, dear,' Lydia says.

'I did? I don't remember...' We wait, silently horrified as another vicious coughing fit takes hold. She looks exhausted when it passes, and her bottom lip is wet with fresh blood. Lydia's hand shakes as she wipes it away.

'I'll hitch the wagon,' Liz says, heading for the door. 'Come with me, John. We're going to Woodland.'

'Where's the pie?' Mary Jane croaks.

'Never mind that,' I say. 'You just rest while we fetch the Doc. He'll fix you up in no time.'

Mary Jane frowns. 'I don't need him. Lord above, we've only just finished paying off the last set of bills . . .'

'Don't be a beef-head,' Lydia snaps. 'Of *course* we're going to get him. Look at the state of you!'

'You'd go if it was one of us falling face-first into a pie,' I say.

Mary Jane looks at me, and a twinkle comes into her eye. 'I was just hungry.'

We laugh, but Mary Jane's quickly turns into another coughing fit.

Mary Jane recovered enough to get upstairs and into her own bed before Liz and John got back with Doc Barker. We're all waiting downstairs around the kitchen table while he examines her. Ma has John on her lap and looks as broken as Mary Jane's pie.

After about a hundred years Doc Barker comes downstairs with his rattling bag. I can tell by his face that the news ain't good.

'I'm sorry to say that Mary Jane has tuberculosis,' he says.

'I feared as much,' Ma groans, 'but she insisted she was all right. She *promised* me she was.'

'What's tuber . . . tuberclorosis?' John asks, looking around with wide eyes.

'Tuberculosis,' Doc Barker says, 'is a disease of the lungs. That's why your sister's been coughing so much.'

'Will she get better?'

'Course she will,' I say firmly. 'Right, Doc?'

'Her condition may well improve enough for her to carry on as usual. She's got grit, and that'll serve her well in that regard.'

'But . . . ?' Lydia says, giving him a hard stare.

The Doc purses his lips. 'Improvement will depend on how she behaves from this moment on. She must rest as much as she can and not tire herself out.'

'We can help her with that,' Liz says.

'Sure, we can take on her chores,' I nod.

'I'm sure you will,' Doc Barker says. 'But whatever happens you must be prepared for the fact that any respite from this disease will be temporary, limited, and followed by an inevitable decline to her health and vigour.'

'Speak plainly, Doc,' Lydia snaps. 'What's going to happen to my sister?'

Doc Barker looks at all of us in turn and says, 'She'll die. I can't say when, but I reckon it'll be a matter of months, if not weeks.'

We sit in stunned silence. Liz slumps down in her chair. 'Isn't there anything you can do?'

'I'm afraid there's no cure for tuberculosis.'

I look up at the ceiling. My voice is barely a whisper. 'Does she know?'

Doc Barker nods. 'She's a clever one. She'd already guessed her affliction and seems to have accepted it in as sanguine a fashion as I've ever seen in all my years practising medicine.'

'But she's only fifteen,' Ma says, her voice distant.

'It's a cruel disease,' the Doc nods, 'and you're not the only family in the county suffering its predations.'

'What can we do for her?' I ask.

'Breathing will get harder as the disease takes hold. Fresh air will help with that. Keep her bedroom window open and take her outside whenever she's able. Try to keep her as rested as possible. No heavy work. Light household duties only from now on.'

'It'll be hard to stop Mary Jane from working,' Liz says.

'Impossible, I'd say,' adds Sarah Ellen.

'Well, you must try, for her sake.'

Ma seems to come back to herself when Doc Barker stands up to leave. 'Liz, fetch my purse.'

He holds up his hand. 'No need this time, Mrs Mosey. I'm just sorry to be the bearer of such bad news.'

11

We're all doing our best to get along as if nothing's changed, and it's Mary Jane who's trying hardest. On good days she's up at her usual early hour. Liz and Sarah Ellen help her wash and dress. I hear them talking through the ceiling over Mary Jane's coughs and then her slow climb down the stairs.

Before, it was Mary Jane who lit the stove, put on the coffee, made the porridge and rousted us all from bed. She was the beginning of our day and she didn't stop looking after us until she went to bed. Now she often can't do anything but slump in a chair with her eyes squeezed shut, holding a bloody handkerchief to her mouth. On other days, the really *bad* days, she's too weak to get up at all and just lies in bed, grey face shiny with sweat, body hardly raising a lump in the blankets.

When the Doc comes every Tuesday we wait downstairs till he's finished. Are we hoping for a miracle? A magical cure? I pray for those things but am always disappointed when I see his grave face.

I sometimes dream there's a monster squatting inside Mary Jane's chest. It squeezes her lungs with rotten fingers, and coughs and rattles and laughs. When I wake up, I imagine lining it up with my rifle and shooting it dead through the heart.

Fall's coming and I did my morning hunt in a steady shower of leaves. I love this time of year. The harvest's in (although it was harder without Mary Jane's help), the weather's still warm and the woods are turning gold. I've come back with two quail (trapped) and a chipmunk (shot) and found Mary Jane sitting at the table reading to John.

My heart lifts. She looks better today. Her skin has a touch of colour, her eyes are bright, and she smiles when she sees me. 'The huntress returns with our supper,' she says. 'What shall I cook, I wonder?'

Lydia pokes her head inside through an open window. 'Nothing,' she says. 'Liz and Sarah Ellen'll make supper. You can supervise, if you must.'

'My, what sharp ears you have, Grandma,' Mary Jane says.

John gives a delighted laugh. 'That's what Red Riding Hood said!'

'I'm glad you were paying attention,' Mary Jane replies. 'But story-time's over. Go fetch the girls and ask them to pluck this haul.' She pushes herself up from the table and holds out an arm for me to take. 'In the meantime, I'm going for a walk with Annie. This fine morning is not to be wasted.'

Arm-in-arm, we make our way over the meadow to the bench beneath a buckeye tree. We sit close, and I hear the sandpaper rasp in Mary Jane's chest.

'I always think of Pa when I sit here.' She takes my hand. 'Will you think of me when I'm gone?'

'There's no need to talk like that,' I frown. 'You're as strong as I've ever seen you . . .'

My words trail off when I see Mary Jane's sad smile. 'Annie dear, you know that's not true. This disease has me in its grip and it won't let go. But I take comfort knowing that I'll be remembered. Fondly, I hope!'

A world without Mary Jane. What will that be like? What will she leave behind? An empty bed. A silent kitchen. A cold stove. Unbearable. Un*bear*able.

I don't know how long I cry for, but she holds me the whole time, hushing and shushing and rocking me back and forth. Eventually my sobs subside into little hitches. I sit back up. My throat feels raw.

'There now,' Mary Jane says. 'Feeling better?'

'No,' I say, digging the heels of my hands into my eyes. 'This is all wrong. It's me who should be comforting you.'

Mary Jane laughs – a sound I want to catch and keep forever.

'Never you mind, young Annie,' she says. 'All I need is for you to be here with me, even if your face is all red and puffy.'

We sit quietly for a while, watching the flycatchers wheel and dive overhead. The donkey brays as John pumps a pail full of water. It's a normal day on the Mosey farm, and it's impossible to believe that my big sister will soon be gone.

'Are you afraid?' I ask.

Mary Jane thinks on this then says, 'Are you going to start crying again, if I tell you the truth?'

'I don't know,' I shrug. 'Probably.'

'It's just I reckon you'll shrivel up like a raisin if you shed any more tears.'

I give a laugh that sounds like a gulp. 'I'll try not to.'

Mary Jane looks down at our entwined hands. I see her pursed lips, the creases in her brow and the tiny blue veins around her eyes; never before has she looked so much like Ma.

'Yes. I'm afraid. Especially at night or when I'm struggling to find my breath. But mostly I'm sad to be leaving you all. I always imagined that we'd grow up together, get married, have children, and share our lives until we were old and grey.'

'It's just so unfair!' Now my tears are hot with fury. 'Of all the people in the world, why is He taking you?'

'I've been asking myself the same thing.' Mary Jane sighs. 'I prayed hard at first. Hard and angrily. Why me? Why'd He make me a lunger? But then I got to thinking. Who am I, a country girl from Ohio, to guess God's plan? He's sure to have His reasons, and I take comfort from that. Maybe Pa's up there feeling lonesome, and God decided he needed one of us to keep him company.'

'That's a nice notion,' I say, although I didn't believe Pa would agree to such a thing.

'Another nice notion is that I'll be able to look down on

you and see what you're up to. So, you'd better behave yourself or I'll come back as a ghost and haunt you in the night!' She pats my hand. 'Now. I'm hungry, so why don't you rustle us up a picnic?'

'All right.'

I glance round as I cross the meadow. Mary Jane's leaning back with her face turned up towards the sun. Perhaps it's the light, but she looks younger, just like before she got sick. Taking that as a good sign, I head to the cabin.

'What are you up to?' Lydia asks as I lay a cloth on the table and heap it with bread, cheese and ham.

'Making a picnic. Come join us. We're on the bench.'

'All right. I'll come up when I've washed my hands.'

After tying up the food in the cloth, I scamper back to the meadow . . . and stop when I see Mary Jane. She's slumped forward on the bench with her chin resting on her chest. Her arms hang limp by her sides. The cloth bag slips from my fingers. Food scatters onto the grass. For a moment I can't stir even a muscle, then I'm flying towards her with the grass whipping my legs.

'Mary Jane,' I cry, 'Not yet – *please*!'

I fall to my knees and weep with relief when my sister stirs and looks at me. 'Oh my . . . I must have nodded off,' she says. 'Whatever's the matter with you, Annie? And where's my lunch? I'm starving.'

12

WINTER 1867

Mary Jane died three months later, during a bitterly cold night in November.

Ma was by her bedside. 'She slipped away in peace, and I thank God I was with her when she did,' she told us the next morning. We all went upstairs to see her, but I don't want to talk about that.

Life's been hazy-grey since the funeral. Without Mary Jane it's like the world's been set at the wrong angle. It's quieter without her singing, colder without her smile, less cheery without her homey, domestic ways.

Ma wakes us up now, but she doesn't have Mary Jane's gentle way about it. Lydia makes the coffee (weaker) and the porridge (lumpier), Liz's pastry decorations look more like monsters than birds, and when I make the beds I never slap and thump the straw mattresses down as smoothly as Mary Jane always did.

Lydia says it's like the sun's gone out. John wanders around like a little lost ghost. Ma's sorrow runs deep but she bears it in silence, for our sakes, I suppose. When I go to the woods I spend more time wandering in despondence than hunting.

We have to work even harder now, from the moment we rise to long after sunset. I'm tired and hungry *all* the time. My hands are hard from the endless scrubbing, sweeping, stone-clearing, cooking and cleaning. And yet, despite all that, we're falling behind. The pantry's nearly bare and the kitchen garden's overgrown. There's a pile of wood that needs chopping and the roof leaks in three places.

Oh, and the pasture's empty because we had to sell dear Pink to pay for Mary Jane's funeral.

Winter's thawed to spring, which has relieved us from the cold if not our grief. It's been another hard day and although I'm exhausted I can't get to sleep. Instead, I lie in bed listening to Ma and Lydia talking at the table.

'I wish we could afford to hire some help,' Ma says, rocking a sleeping Huldie in her arms.

'I wish we could fix the plough. It's about ready to fall apart.' Lydia's chair creaks as she leans back. 'And poor Maple's getting too old to pull the darn thing. Way things are going, we won't be able to bring in a full harvest this year. If we're not careful the bank will foreclose and the bailiffs will turn us out into the road.'

I don't know what 'foreclose' means, or what 'bailiffs' are, but the mere mention of them turns Ma pale. 'Heaven forbid,' she says. 'Oh, the shame of it. We'd end up living in the Infirmary like beggars.'

'It'd be better than starving.'

'Lydia!'

'Well, it's true. When was the last time any of us had enough to eat? I'm hungry and shaky all the time, so Lord knows how you're feeling. I know you give most of your portions to John and Huldie.'

Ma gives an angry shake of her head. 'I don't need much. Never have.'

'Fiddle faddle. You used to eat more than Pa.' Lydia sighs. 'No matter what we do, there's never enough to go around.'

I slip out from the blankets and pad over to Ma into the kitchen, expecting to be ordered straight back to bed. Instead, Ma draws me close and kisses my forehead. 'What's the matter, Phoebe? Can't sleep?'

I shake my head. 'I was listening. I want to help.'

'You do more than your share with your hunting,' Lydia says as I drag out a chair and sit down.

'I can hunt for longer, dig more traps . . .'

'I'm afraid that won't be enough to stop the slide.' Lydia's eyes are fixed on Ma. 'We're going to have to make some hard choices.'

Ma looks down at Huldie. A tear rolls down her nose.

When she speaks, her words are so quiet I can barely hear them: 'Who'll take her?'

'The Fairheads might,' Lydia says. 'God's not blessed them with a child.'

'They're decent, church-going folk, I suppose.'

'They are. They'll take care of her.'

I look back and forth between them. 'You mean you're . . . giving Huldie away?'

'I'm afraid so,' Lydia says.

'But . . . for how long?'

Ma's face crumples. She gets up with Huldie held tight against her chest, walks to the window and stares out at the darkness. Stray grey locks hang loose from her bun. Her back, usually so straight, is stooped.

'We don't want to,' Lydia says to me. 'But things being the way they are . . . Huldie will be better off with a family who can look after her properly.'

'Keep her warm,' Ma whispers. 'Keep her well.'

'Exactly,' Lydia says. 'Fatten her up, right, Ma?'

Ma bows her head and starts to cry. I get up to go to her, but Lydia grabs my hand and shakes her head. I sit back down, all twisted up inside. I've already lost Pa and Mary Jane, and now I'm to say goodbye to Huldie?

'It's for the best,' Lydia continues. 'The Fairheads are prospering, which means they'll be able to give her a proper education.'

My throat feels thick. 'But she'll forget about us . . .'

Ma spins around. 'No! We're passing Huldie to another family, not losing her altogether.'

'And I'll make sure the Fairheads agree we can visit whenever we want,' Lydia adds.

Ma returns to the table. 'This family is being tested, but if we keep faith with God we'll make it through to the other side.' She sighs and passes Huldie to me. 'I'm exhausted. Put her down for me when you go to bed, would you? And don't stay up too late.'

'We'll go see the Fairheads in the morning?' Lydia says, eyebrows raised.

Ma nods and creaks slowly up the stairs.

I look down at my little sister and try to imagine life without her tottering around the cabin and laughing when we pull faces at her. 'Can I have her with me tonight?'

'I don't see why not.' Lydia takes the dirty cups and puts them in the sink. 'But keep her between you and John so she doesn't roll off the bed.'

'All right.'

Lydia draws a chair close, sits down and leans against me. 'I'm going to miss this little bundle,' she says, rubbing a finger down Huldie's cheek.

I think about how fast and badly things have changed since that terrible winter's night.

'Lydia?'

'Mmm?'

'Do you think the rest of us will manage to stay together?'

'I can't say, Annie dear. But I promise I'm going to do all I can to make sure we do.'

I give a firm nod. 'Me too.'

13

Mr and Mrs Fairhead came by today and took Huldie away.

Ma had tried to explain to her that she was going to live with a new family who had a big house in Greenville where she'd have her very own room, and that they'd love her just as much as we do.

But Huldie's only three and didn't understand. Not when Ma packed all her clothes into a bag and placed Sophie the doll on top. Not when the Fairheads came into the cabin, looking excited and awkward at the same time. Not even when, one by one, we hugged Huldie and kissed her goodbye.

Dear Huldie only began to realise when Ma, looking grey and shattered, handed her to Mrs Fairhead and we all trooped outside and lined up on the porch. She watched us from over Mrs Fairhead's shoulder. At first she looked confused, but when they clambered up into the pony and trap next to Mr Fairhead, her eyes widened and she looked terrified.

Mr Fairhead turned to us, but before he could speak my sister started to struggle and squirm so hard that Mrs Fairhead nearly dropped her. Huldie's half-cry, half-scream cut right through to my heart. Ma gave a low moan and took a step forward. Liz scooped up a snivelling John and carried him back inside. Lydia took mine and Sarah Ellen's hands.

Over Huldie's wretched cries I heard Mrs Fairhead urge her husband to go, and I know I'll never forget the sight of Ma watching them ride away, with one hand clamped over her mouth as if trying to stifle a scream.

I went straight to the woods after that.

I know Huldie ain't dead like Pa and Mary Jane, and I know she's better off with rich folk. Even so, my sadness is as raw as a freshly skinned knee, and it'll pain me for a long while yet. I love my little sister from tip to toe, and I'm going to miss her – heck, I already *do* miss her – more than I could ever say.

But here in the woods, away from the grief and tears, surrounded by trees and the whispering leaves, I find my breath more easily.

I know pretty much every tree in the woods around our farm. There's one, an oak a fair ways in, that stands in a clearing. It looks healthy with its wide sky-reaching branches, 'cept for the fact that there's an ugly hole reaching deep into the trunk. I don't know what caused it – disease maybe – but to me it looks like something has reached inside and torn that poor oak's heart right out.

That's how the cabin feels these days.

Months have passed since we lost Huldie, and even though we promised to go and see her, we hardly ever do, and *never* all together. The Fairheads live in Greenville, which is too far away to walk, and we have to save poor Maple's legs for farm work.

Truth be told, things don't seem much better even without Huldie to feed. We still get up at dawn and do three hours' housework before breakfast. Then it's outside whatever the weather to feed Maple, trek to buy eggs and milk from the Maslens, wash our clothes in the creek, work the fields, tend the garden, and pick wild berries and mushrooms. On top of that I go to the woods to check my traps and try to bag a bird or two with my rifle.

I'm a daisy shot to be sure, but I'm having to learn the best way to track and hunt on my own. And I ain't going to lie: it's a challenge. Especially when I'm so weak from hunger that it's hard to hold the rifle steady. I'd say I bring something back every second or third trip out.

Anyway, all this means that despite our aching muscles, creaking bones and calloused hands, we still go hungry and have no money to spare even for gunpowder and shot.

14

MIDSUMMER 1870

I've woken early, so rather than lie in bed stewing in worry, I'm going to do something useful. The sky's pale blue behind the trees but the cabin's still dark. I light a candle. Then I fetch my hunting bag, sit at the kitchen table, spread out the things I need and set to work. I've had so much practice now that it takes me no time to make perfect cartridges; I believe I could even do it blindfolded.

First, I fold squares of paper into tubes. Second, I pour in the exact right amount of gunpowder. Third, I drop in a bullet. And finally, I twist the top shut so everything's held inside nice and tight. I like this job. It's satisfying. To get good takes practice, and I believe that I've now got it down to what Pa called a 'fine art'.

I make an even dozen, slot them neatly into the bag and retrieve the long rifle from over the fireplace. It's a bit frustrating that even though I'm ten years old I still have to stand on a chair to reach. I'd love to be tall like how Mary Jane was, but Lydia says I'm as big as I'm ever going to be, and I need to prepare for the day I start shrinking.

I creep from the cabin and head up the lane with the rifle over my shoulder. The sun's broken free from the trees, but there's still a few scraps of mist drifting about and a cold edge in the air. My spirits lift as a yellow hooded warbler flutters from the trees and disappears over the corn fields.

I whistle softly as I load my rifle in the shadow of the woods. I hardly need to think about it any more, each action comes natural as breathing. Then, carrying it half-cocked and at the ready, I step through the tree line into deep green gloom. Here, in the woods, I know my task and how to do it. Here, in the woods, I can forget the woes and worries of the outside and think about something else for a while.

I follow my senses like a hunting cat: silent, wide-eyed, alert. Is that a new rabbit trail to my left? The chatter of a chipmunk above? A whiff of fox scat on the breeze? I take in every sight, sound and smell, chew them over, and decide my best path to catch me some game.

Deeper into the trees I go, heading for the closest trap. I see straightaway that I might've gotten lucky. The grain I'd left around the edge has gone and the straw's fallen into the hole. I peer inside and find a sleeping quail. After a quick thank-you prayer, I wring the bird's neck and hang it from my belt. I savour the relief. We won't go hungry tonight.

But I'm not finished yet.

There's a clearing to the west that the turkeys seem to like. It's quite a way and I'll be late back to the cabin, but I want to be by myself for a spell. I follow the creek as it rushes through roots and shines rocks to a sparkle. After a while the trees thin out and I'm wading through hip-high patches of swaying grass and surrounded by the *creek-creek-creek* of crickets. I turn my face to the sun, as Mary Jane loved to, and soak up the warmth.

Lydia's told me many times that she'd love to live in a city like Cincinnati, where there's lots of bustle and bright lights. I'd like to travel too, see the world beyond the horizon. But I know that whatever exciting things I see and folks I meet, my heart will always be here in the woods of Ohio.

The clearing's ahead. I slow down, taking care not to tread on any sticks, and kneel behind a tree. My luck's holding. There's three turkeys strutting around in the open. I choose the biggest, line him up, give a soft whistle through my teeth so he looks up, and pull the trigger.

My target drops in a little explosion of feathers. The gunshot echoes through the trees; the other birds scatter; smoke drifts. Thankful that the turkey didn't suffer, I pick him up and set off home. I'm halfway down the track when I see Ma heading towards me . . . and there's something about her expression that makes me uneasy.

'Morning, Ma.'

'Morning, Phoebe. I was just coming up to find you. That's a fine-looking bird.' She smiles, but it looks forced. 'Go hang it up in the barn and meet me in the meadow.'

I do as she asks, wondering what this is about. The grass in the meadow is knee high and the wild flowers rampant without Pink's grazing. My legs are damp with dew by the time I find Ma sitting on the stone water trough.

'I miss Pink,' I say, watching a ladybug crawl over my hand. 'She always liked it when we came visiting.'

'I miss her milk and cream,' Ma says, 'but we've got the Maslens for that now.'

Bees drone and clamber over the flowers. A gentle breeze hisses through the grass. Cotton boll clouds hang over the woods. It'd be oh-so-peaceful if not for Ma's fidgeting, frowning and picking at loose threads on her dress. My unease curdles to worry. Are we expecting bailiffs (who I now know are men who take your belongings if you can't pay your debts)? Is someone sick?

'What is it, Ma?'

Without looking up, Ma says, 'It's going to be a tough winter for the Moseys. The worst ever, I expect. Only half a harvest, a broken plough and a horse who can barely haul. I've got bills piling up and the larder's so bare it makes me want to weep.'

'So, we work harder.'

Ma shakes her head. 'How can we work harder? We're doing all we can, but we won't have enough money or food to see all of us through the winter.'

My stomach does a flop when I realise what she's driving at. Who's being sent away this time? John? Liz? Sarah Ellen?

When Ma turns to me with glistening eyes, I know she means me.

15

LATE SUMMER, 1870

I'm lying in bed, staring up at the rafters and listening to familiar night-time sounds: John's snores, the wind sighing around the eaves, the *tick-tick-tick* of the cooling stove, and although I'm tired I *must not* let myself fall sleep. If I do, the morning I've been dreading for weeks will arrive too quickly.

My bag's by the cabin door. Liz and Sarah Ellen helped me pack it last night. Afterwards they hugged me and said how much they would miss me, and that they'd come visit whenever they could. But the Infirmary in Greenville is a fifty-mile round trip, so I don't think I'll see them very often.

It's still dark outside, but the cardinals, chickadees and bluebirds are starting to sing. I normally love the sound, but not today. Birds, go back to sleep! And then, perhaps, the sun won't rise, the morning won't come, and I won't have to go.

Ma told me that of all her children she'd chosen me to send away because my wild and independent ways would help me. That she knew I'd stand on my own two feet because I'd been doing so since I was a little scrap who loved to run off on her own and not return until covered in mud and scratches, and bursting with news about fox dens or birds' nests or strange mushrooms I'd discovered.

But I don't feel strong. Not at *all*. I feel small and full of dread for what's lurking down the road. I already feel alone, even though I've not left home.

Light creeps through the windows. A cock crows in the distance. I slip from the bed and go outside. There's only a few stars left and the treetops to the east are tipped with gold. I skirt around the cabin and into the kitchen garden, which smells of mint, basil and thyme, then wade in the stream where we wash. I say goodbye to the barn cats and give Maple a final groom.

I feel like a restless spirit as I flit from one familiar place to another, wondering how long it will be before I see them again.

My face is scrubbed, I'm wearing my best dress and my straw hat with the feather on it, my boots are laced up tight, and Ma's brushed and tied my hair with yellow ribbons. 'I want you looking your best when you meet Mr and Mrs Edington,' she says, 'and do us Moseys proud.'

Liz peers out through the window. 'Wagon's ready. Lydia's waiting.'

We all head out. Lydia gives Maple a pat and joins us. No one speaks and I guess they're feeling as sick and sad as I am.

'Well,' Ma eventually says, 'it's time to say goodbye. Go on, John. You first.'

John steps close, eyes downcast. 'Bye, Annie. I made this for you.' He holds out a piece of wood that he's whittled.

'Well now, isn't this lovely?' I say, trying to work out what it's supposed to be.

'It's a turkey,' he tells me (much to my relief). 'You know, because of your hunting.'

'I love it,' I say truthfully, giving him a long, hard hug. 'Thank you.'

Liz and Sarah Ellen step forward together. 'We've been saving up and we got you this.' Liz holds out a little wooden box and flips up the lid. It's full of coloured cotton reels, a set of needles and a thimble, all set in their own compartments.

'And we sent away for this magazine of embroidery patterns,' Sarah Ellen adds. 'It came all the way from New York. It's mostly birds and animals. We thought you'd like that one best.'

I take the box and magazine and slip them carefully into my bag. 'Thank you,' I say, 'but you shouldn't have—'

I'm suddenly enveloped.

'We'll miss you, dear Annie . . .'

'You must think of us often . . .'

'We'll pray for you every night . . .'

'And we'll see you soon.'

I feel safe in their arms and I don't want them to let go.

But they do, and I feel like a snail that's had its shell ripped off.

Ma's sitting by the pump. She beckons me over and draws me onto her lap. She smells, as always, of soap.

'Now then, I have something for you too.' She passes me the framed photograph that stands on her bedside table. It shows Ma sitting on a chair holding me when I was a baby. Pa's standing behind with a hand on her shoulder. 'We had this taken after you were born. I want you to have it.'

'Thanks, Ma.' My throat feels tight and my voice is wavering.

'Why don't we make a promise,' she says, 'that we'll get another photograph taken when we're all together again.'

'When will that be?'

'I don't know, dear, but we will. I promise. And until that moment, I'm trusting in God to look after you. Now then, you'd better get along. It's a long way to the Infirmary and I don't want Lydia travelling back in the dark.'

I want to be brave so I give her a smile and a kiss on the cheek. But I'm only pretending. I've never in my whole life felt more afraid. It takes every last scrap of courage just to slide off Ma's lap and drag myself over to the wagon, where Lydia waits in the driver's seat.

She picks up the reins. 'Ready?'

'No,' I whisper.

'I know,' she says. 'None of us are.'

She flicks the reins and the wagon trundles off. Liz, Sarah Ellen and John trot after us. Ma follows behind, arms stiff at her sides. They stop at the gate, waving and shouting their goodbyes. I wave back, twisting awkwardly in the seat, and I don't turn away until the wagon rounds a bend and they're lost to sight.

The midday sun gleams from a bright blue sky. Golden wheat sways in the fields. It's such a beautiful day, and I can't stop crying.

16

I must have fallen asleep because the next thing I know Lydia's shaking me and saying, 'We're here.'

The wagon's stopped on the side of the road near what I'm guessing is the outskirts of Greenville – certainly nowhere near where the Fairheads and Huldie live. I jump as a two-wheeled trap rattles past. An ox-hauled cart laden with barrels grinds up the other side of the road; the driver tips his hat to us as he passes.

Ahead, the road becomes a busy street lined with wooden buildings, some with names painted in large letters on the walls. They're too far away for me to see, but I'm guessing they'll be saloons, hotels, barbershops, restaurants and stores. Oooh, maybe a gunsmith . . . I hear distant town-sounds: voices, shouts, hammering, hoofbeats. Bells chime from a large white church.

I feel rumpled, groggy and queasy with nerves. I rub my eyes and put my hat back on straight. 'Where . . . ?'

Lydia points. 'Over there.'

Set a fair way back from the road is the biggest building

I've ever seen. It's made of brick and looks down on me through more dark windows than I can count (so, more than twenty). It could not be more different from our cosy, crooked little cabin.

'Oh my,' I whisper as we clamber to the ground.

'I know it looks a bit . . . uninviting,' Lydia says, 'but Mr and Mrs Edington are the nicest couple you'll ever meet. And look' – she points over the picket fence – 'the grounds back right onto woods you can go tramping about in. It'll be just like home.'

I nod, but Lydia's cheerful voice sounds about as real as a three-dollar bill.

There's a house and stables near the treeline, separate from the Infirmary but still in the grounds. A horse peers out from one of the half-doors. 'Is that where the Edingtons live?'

'I guess so.' Lydia takes down my bag. 'And I daresay they'll teach you to ride if you do right by them.'

'That'd be daisy. Means I'll be able to come visit more often.'

'You sure could.' She gives me a tight smile and hands me my bag. 'Come on then. Let's get you settled in.'

'No. Let's say goodbye out here, in the sun where it's more cheerful.'

Lydia frowns. 'You sure?'

'Yeah. Anyway, you should get going or you'll be riding back in the dark.'

'All right.' She looks away and I see she's *this close* to crying. 'Annie, I . . . I'm sorry. I'm the eldest and it should be me coming here, not you.'

'Now *there's* a foolish notion. You know as well as I that Ma needs you to look after the farm, John's too sensitive to be sent away, and can you even imagine splitting up Liz and Sarah Ellen?'

Lydia sniffs and shakes her head. 'They'd be lost without each other.'

'Exactly. It has to be me.' I give her a smile. 'Don't look so gloomy. It's not a becoming look for a lady-about-town and esteemed visitor to the White House such as yourself.'

'You're *so* right. I'm expecting another invitation from President Grant any day now.'

'Well, of *course*, for we were *such* entertaining company last time.'

'I will send for you when it arrives.'

'Please do.'

Our smiles fade. She takes my hands. 'Look after yourself.'

'Sure will. And don't let my rifle get dusty.'

'Sure won't.' She climbs up onto the wagon. 'Bye, Annie.'

'Bye, Lydia.'

I watch her drive away. My queasiness darkens to dread the moment she's out of sight, and I have to fight the urge to race after her. The road's gotten busier. Carts clatter, horses clop, people laugh and shout. I gasp as a mangy dog nearly gets mangled under a wagon, then step aside as a trio of sweaty workmen push past with barrows piled with tools and pails.

I step through the Infirmary gate and gaze up at all those windows. Most are blank, 'cept for a few sad faces peering out. One, a little girl with hollow eyes and a slack mouth, ducks back when she sees me looking. A young couple in threadbare clothes stand close in the shade of a maple tree. He talks quietly, urgently, until the woman gives a cry of disgust, throws up her hands and storms away. The man's boot heel flaps as he hurries after her.

Ma always spoke about this place with fear, as if ending up here was the very worst thing that could happen. It was something to be ashamed of, to avoid at all costs. Yet here I am . . . I stare at the front door. It's only ten steps away, but I can't move. I realise it's not the building that's making my stomach churn and my throat tight. It's who waits inside.

Strangers.

Come on. Let's get it over with. Gravel crunches under my feet. I glance through a window as I climb the porch steps and see a family group sitting in a gloomy huddle surrounded by bags and suitcases.

I look up at the door and wonder why they made it so darn tall. Do giants live here? I rap my knuckles against it, but the wood's so thick it hardly makes a sound. Banging my fist don't work either. I shuffle about for a while, not sure what to do, until I finally lose patience.

'For heaven's sake, Annie,' I mutter, 'stop being so yellow and get on with it!'

I reach for the brass door handle, figuring if it's locked I'll march round the back to find another entrance. But the handle turns, and with a shove, the door opens.

17

Floorboards with their polish long-since worn away to the edges creak as I step into a hallway lined with dark wood panels, doorways and unlit lanterns. I wrinkle my nose at the smell of soap, dirty laundry and boiled vegetables. A staircase leads up to a landing with yet more doors and passages. I halt on the doormat, unwilling to delve deeper into this rambling place that feels so big, yet at the same time close and confining.

Apart from the gloomy family in a room to my right, I can't see anybody. But the sounds of people are all around: the clash of pots and pans from somewhere deep in the back (the kitchen, probably), shouts, footsteps.

'Excuse me,' I call down the empty hallway. 'I'm looking for Mrs Edington—'

I nearly jump out of my skin when a member of the gloomy family says something in a language I don't understand and slams the door. Keeping the front door open as an escape route, I head towards the stairs. I'm just wondering why I'm trying to be quiet even though I want to attract attention, when I'm startled (again!) by thumping footsteps overhead.

A ragged little boy with wild hair and no shoes hurtles round the bannisters and bounds down the stairs two at a time. I'm about to cry 'Be careful!' when he slips, tumbles and lands in a heap at my feet. For an awful moment I think he might have brained himself, but then, to my relief, he starts to wail.

'There now,' I say, kneeling next to him. 'What a nasty fall. Where's it hurt?'

'*Every*where!'

'Oh dear,' I say, checking to see if any of his limbs are facing the wrong way. 'Tell me where it hurts the most, then.'

'On my leeeeeg!' he says, thrashing about like a landed fish.

'All right . . . Try to stay still while I look . . .'

'What's all the commotion?' a voice calls from where I guess the kitchen is. A tall, willowy woman wiping soap-sudsy hands on her apron marches down the hallway towards us. A bunch of keys rattles on her belt. 'Oh, James,' she says in a voice that's equal parts exasperated and concerned. 'What have you done now?'

'I . . . *sob* . . . fell . . . *sob* . . . down . . .'

'The stairs,' the woman sighs. 'For the second time in as many days.'

'He says it's his leg.'

The woman, who I guess is Mrs Edington, gives him a quick and practised examination. 'Twisted ankle. You're lucky it's not a broken neck.' She picks him up and marches up the stairs as if he's no heavier than a pillow, then stops and looks down at me. 'Come on then. Work to do!'

I'm about to follow when she adds, 'You'd better bring your bag. Not all my residents will resist the temptation of larceny.'

I guess 'larceny' means stealing so I grab my bag and hurry up the stairs. I stop on the landing and look around. Where is she? She could have gone down any one of these passageways . . . It's lighter up here. Dust floats in front of a large window. I see an elderly woman, face wrinkled and brown as old leather, folding sheets in a room piled high with laundry.

I follow the sound of jangling keys and find Mrs Edington in a dormitory of ten beds, each with a wooden chest at its foot. She lays the snivelling James on a bed near a window and draws up a chair.

'Now then, James, Phoebe's going to hold your hand while I check your ankle, so just lie still.' She raises her gaze to me. 'You are Phoebe Mosey, aren't you? Have I guessed that correct?'

'Yes, Ma'am,' I say, taking James' hand. 'But I prefer Annie, if you don't mind.'

'I don't. I'm Mrs Edington. My husband and I are the superintendents of the Darke County Infirmary.' James winces as she runs her hands over his ankle. 'Mmm, quite a nasty strain. Which would never have happened if you were in class with Mr Edington as you were supposed to be.' She waves a hand over her shoulder. 'Annie, be a dear and fetch me a bandage from that cupboard, would you?'

I do as she asks and watch as she wraps James' ankle with as much speed and gentleness as Mary Jane ever did for me. 'Now,' she says, 'if you get out of bed your foot's likely to fall clean off' – James gives a little gasp – 'so you stay here until I come back. Annie, come with me.'

'Bye, James,' I say. 'I'll stop by and see you later.'

I follow Mrs Edington up two flights of stairs and into a tiny bedroom with a sloping ceiling. I put my bag down as she opens the curtains and lets in a shaft of afternoon sunlight.

'This is your room,' she says. 'Small, I know, but it's quiet up here.'

'My room? You mean . . . all to myself?'

Mrs Edington smiles. 'We might be overcrowded but we don't make our residents share beds.' She plops down on a chair and gives an almighty sigh. 'What a day. A family arrived this morning. Evicted from their farm, poor things, and I still don't know where we can put them. It'll be the stable at this rate. And what with James' monkeyshines . . . Anyway, I'm glad you're here to lend a hand.'

'Who else lives here?' The bed squeaks as I take a perch.

'Oh, all sorts. County folk who've fallen on hard times. Vagrants, the feeble-minded, old timers with no one to look after them. The sick, the poor.'

'The poor,' I murmur. 'Like me.'

'Well, poverty's nothing to be ashamed of. Sometimes things get so tough folk need a bit of help, so they come here.'

I glance through the window at the trees backing onto the Infirmary grounds. 'If you like, I can set traps in those woods, bring some game in for you.'

'Ah, yes. Your ma said you were quite the hunter.' She looks at me keenly. 'I daresay we could use some fresh meat, but most of your work will be in and around the Infirmary, cooking, cleaning, helping with the children. Can you sew?'

'A little. I can darn too.'

'Good. There's always needlework to be done. I can teach you embroidery, as well. Oh, and Mr Edington will want to see you in class a few times a week. We do our best to educate the children, even tearaways like James.' She blows out her cheeks and stands up. 'Right, back to work. You get settled then come find me in the kitchen.'

I'd prepared for the worst, but in the end this place don't seem so bad. Mrs Edington's all right, and I'm sure she'll let me take a day off here and there to visit home. I hum as I unpack my bag. The last item is John's whittled wood. I place it on the bedside table, and you know what? From some angles, it *does* look a bit like a turkey.

PART TWO

18

MID-FALL 1870

I'm woken up as usual by the clatter of empty churns as Mr Edington makes his way to the cowshed to milk the Infirmary herd. I jump out of bed, put on my work dress (which Mrs Edington helped me embroider with flowers and birds last week), stockings and boots.

I'm already looking forward to breakfast. Everyone here gets fed three times a day, and I've certainly gotten stronger in the weeks since arriving. Breakfast is coffee, porridge and *cornbread*, my new favourite food. It's golden brown and tastes best straight from the oven. A resident called Mrs Stone makes it. She's from Tennessee and she's got this real slow way of speaking. 'Stretching words like treacle from a spoon,' Mr Edington says. Mrs Stone cries a lot, and never goes anywhere without a battered ragdoll tucked into her belt.

Truth be told, the Infirmary's a sad place full of people who've hit hard times and have nowhere else to go. I try to be cheerful, even when I'm tired and missing home. After two months here I know most of the residents by name, and they certainly know me because I'm forever running around and being a general helper around the place. I've hardly had a chance to explore the woods, let alone set any traps. Maybe I'll be able to venture out this Sunday after prayers.

I'm hurrying downstairs to the kitchen, saying 'Good morning' to everyone, when I run into Mrs Edington. 'Ah, Annie,' she says. 'Just the person I wanted to see. Come with me, I have some news for you.' I follow her into her office, wondering – hoping – if Ma has sent for me to come home.

'Now then,' Mrs Edington says, sitting down behind a paper-strewn desk. 'I had a letter last month from a local farmer asking if we have anyone suitable to help his wife with their new baby, and I suggested you.'

'Me? But I've so much to do around here . . . How often will I be helping them?'

'No, you don't understand,' she says. 'What I mean is you'll be moving in with them. Living there. Permanently.'

I stare at her. 'You're sending me away?'

'Well, I wouldn't put it *quite* like that, Annie.'

'But that's what you're doing,' I say, feeling my cheeks flush. 'I don't want to leave. I'm starting to like it here, helping with the children and such . . .'

'It's partly your way with the children that put you in mind.' Her face softens. 'I know it's sudden, but I think you'd be better off with a family. I met Mr Grace – and isn't that a nice name? – and, although he's a man of few words, I believe he's decent, hardworking and wants what's best for his family.'

I look down at my boots as dread for the unknown seeps into my stomach. 'How far away does he live? Can I still come and visit?'

'Per*haps*,' she replies. 'I said local, but the Graces do live a fair way away. But listen, I've not said the best part yet. I told Mr Grace what a good shot you are, and he said you'd be able to go hunting whenever you wanted. They live way out in the country, so there'll be plenty of game.'

I chew on that morsel. 'Do you know what sort of guns he has?'

'I'm afraid I didn't ask,' Mrs Edington smiles. 'But consider this, rather than being cooped up here you'll be out in the country with new places to explore. *And* Mr Grace is going to send two dollars every two weeks to your ma as payment for your work. Imagine the difference that will make.'

I nod and say, 'All right then.'

'Wonderful! That's agreed then.'

Huh. As if I had a choice.

19

My room's empty, my bag's packed, and I'm standing outside Mrs Edington's office waiting to meet Mr Grace. All I know so far is that he has a deep voice and doesn't say much. S'far as I can tell, Mrs Edington's doing most of the talking. I jump when the door opens. She ushers me inside.

'Well, here she is, Mr Grace. Phoebe Mosey. Although you prefer Annie, don't you, dear?'

The office ain't as bright as normal because there's a man in shabby work clothes leaning against the windowsill and blocking the fall sun. He bends forward and peers at me with pale, protruding eyes. 'She's small. Heavy work on a farm.'

Piqued, I speak before Mrs Edington can. 'I grew up on a farm. I can milk cows, plough, sow and reap. There ain't nothing outdoors I can't do.'

'You'll be looking after my daughter mostly,' he replies. 'My wife too. She's had trouble since the birth.'

'Having seen Annie work these past months, I've no doubt she'll be a great help to you,' Mrs Edington says. 'I'll be sorry to lose her.'

Mr Grace keeps his eyes on me. 'You packed?'

'Yes, sir.'

'Then let's go. We've a long journey ahead.' He jams his bowler onto a mess of curly black hair. 'I'm obliged to you, Mrs Edington.'

'I'm glad to help. I think this has worked out well for all of us.'

Mrs Edington leads the way out of the office and as Mr Grace passes, I catch a whiff of something sharp coming off him. Animal dung of some kind? Hogs, maybe.

I follow heavily, reluctantly. I don't want to leave my new home and go to a strange and faraway place. But what can I do? They're grown-ups and I have to do as I'm told. I traipse outside and find he's already waiting on a battered old cart loaded up with sacks of potatoes and chicken feed.

Mrs Edington gives me a quick hug and slips some sandwiches into my bag. 'I know being moved from pillar to post isn't easy, Annie,' she says, 'but this should be the last stop for a long while. You'll be better off in a family home, I promise.'

I can't form any words, so I just nod and climb up into the seat next to Mr Grace. He flicks the reins to set his chestnut horse trotting, and before I know it Mrs Edington and the Infirmary are disappearing into the distance.

I don't know how long we've been driving but he's still not said a word.

We're creaking down a rough road hemmed in by smallholdings, fallow fields and patches of woodland. Greenville's just a brown smudge on the horizon, and there's not many people this far out of town. Mr Grace is wide, so I'm pressing myself against the side of the bench to avoid touching him; that hog smell has lodged in my nostrils and's beginning to make me feel ill.

If only he'd just *say* something! I suppose I could start . . . I know that's what Lydia would do. Oh well, here goes . . .

'That's a fine horse. A Morgan, ain't it?'

He looks askance at me. 'How'd you know that?'

'Oh, my sister, Mary Jane, she taught me lots about horses. She had a book about 'em with lots of pictures.'

He grunts, fishes in his pocket and jams a wad of tobacco into his cheek.

Encouraged to have dragged a few words from him, I try again. 'What's her name?'

'The nag? Betsy.'

'Do you think I'll be able to ride her? I'm pretty good now, even without a saddle. I learned on Maple. That's our horse. We mostly use her for ploughing, but she's getting too old for that now.'

'Mm. Ready for the glue factory, then.'

I shoot him a glare for that. I know what happens to horses when they get too old to work, but it seems thoughtless of him to mention it in such an off-hand fashion.

'S'far as you riding this one, best not, I reckon. She's pretty ornery. Likes to bite. Only listens to me.'

'Oh.'

A new silence drags on until I just can't bear it any more. 'How far's it to your farm?'

'A fair way yet.'

Not a satisfying answer. 'How many miles do you reckon it is from Woodland?'

He thinks for a moment. 'S'about thirty to Greenville. Don't know about Woodland. Never been.'

Pa once told me that it was around twenty-five miles from Woodland to Greenville. I close my eyes to concentrate and came up with the almost unimaginable distance of fifty-five miles.

'Woodland,' he muses. 'That where your people live?'

My people, who are getting further away with every hoofbeat.

'Yes,' I say, but it comes out in a whisper.

'What's that?'

'I said, yes.'

Mr Grace nods his head. 'Yep, a fair old way.'

'What have you got on the farm?'

'Cows, chickens. I'm fattening up some hogs for slaughter.'

So, I was right about the smell. 'I've not looked after hogs before.'

'Gotta be careful with 'em.' He gives me a sidelong look.

'They'll trample a sapling like you flat. Leave them grunters to me. It's Eliza you'll be seeing to.'

'Eliza. That your daughter?'

He nods. 'The most perfect thing I ever seen.'

His surprisingly sentimental answer causes some of the knots in my stomach to unravel enough for me to realise I'm actually quite hungry. I take the sandwiches Mrs Edington made from my bag.

'What you got there?'

'Sandwiches.' I lift up a corner. 'Cheese and ham. D'you want one?'

He nods, spits out his tobacco, and we munch in silence – a silence I don't mind as much as before.

'Can you write?' he asks.

'A little. My sister taught me some.'

'I'm no good at it, but Mrs Grace is clever like that. She'll be able to help you write letters to your people. Let them know how you're doing.'

'Oh, I'd be obliged,' I say.

'I don't want them worrying about you.' He nods ahead. 'This is our turning.'

20

Mr Grace turns the cart onto a narrow track that's so rutted it makes the suspension squeal like a bunch of angry rats. Branches entwine over our heads, blocking the sun and turning the air chilly enough for goosebumps to form on my arms. Rotting leaves carpet the ground. I delve into my bag, pull out a shawl and wrap it around my shoulders.

The track winds deep into the forest. I'm hoping there'll be homesteads or farmhouses, anything to show there are other folk nearby, but all I see are endless trees, bramble thickets and streams filled with sluggish brown water. Can't hear any birds either. It's like winter's come two months early.

'Where's the nearest town?'

Mr Grace, eyes shadowed under his heavy brow, jerks his thumb over his shoulder. 'Back that way and south. Doubt you'll have a need to go there.'

The track straightens. Through the thinning trees I see the last rays of the sun fall on the face of a large wooden farmhouse. It stands on a rise, overlooking a dung-strewn yard, several acres of scrubby pasture and a fenced-off field with half a dozen black-and-white Holstein cows. The farmhouse looks quite grand, with a pitched roof, dark windows and a pillared porch. Betsy speeds up – probably glad to be home after such a long journey – and halts by the front door.

There's outbuildings backing onto the forest – a stable with a slumped roof, a filthy cowshed, what I'm guessing is a feed store, and a smokehouse with oily fumes drifting from the chimney. The cart lurches as Mr Grace jumps down and sets about unhitching the horse. I hesitate for a moment then slip to the ground.

Now that I'm closer, I see the farmhouse ain't so grand after all. It must have been red once, but it's rash-pink and flaky now. There's wall planks missing, and those that ain't hang at the wrong angles, and are cracked and curling where nails have come loose. The windows are edged green with moss, and inside there's more cobweb than curtain. A baby wails somewhere. That must be Eliza. My spirits sink. I don't like this place.

The sun's nearly set. Shadows cast from the surrounding trees creep towards me across the yard. I trot to the side of the house for a peek round the back. A wire-and-wood frame nailed around a twisted old walnut tree is home to a bedraggled bunch of chickens. Beyond lies what I guess used to be a kitchen garden, but is now an overgrown battlefield of shrubs, herbs and weeds. The rest of the space, right up to the surrounding trees, is one huge pen full of clotted mud and rootling hogs.

I'm just coming back to get my bag from the cart when I spot a woman staring at me through one of the farmhouse windows. She's gone before I can wave, then reappears at the front door holding a baby against her chest. Skinny and stooped she may be, but there's wiry strength beneath her tattered dress. It's then that I notice, with a kind of creeping horror, that she's got no shoes on, only filthy stockings with holes in the toes.

After giving me the coldest of appraisals she turns to Mr Grace, who so far has ignored her. 'Where've you been?' she snaps. 'I've been waiting.'

'Mrs Edington kept me,' he replies while undoing the last of Betsy's harness straps. 'Turns out she jaws worse'n you.'

'Or maybe you went to the saloon in Greenville to get slewed on money we ain't got!'

Mr Grace turns on her. 'And what if I did bend my elbow?' he growls. 'S'you that drives me to it.'

My stomach's doing somersaults. I want to crawl away and hide. Are they *always* like this? I flinch when she whips her face towards me.

'This is her, is it?'

'It is.'

She sidles real close; we're eye-to-eye, nose-to-nose, and I only just stop myself retreating from her sour-milk smell.

Despite her straggly hair and sallow skin, I'm guessing she's only about thirty.

'There's nothing of her.' She grabs my arm and squeezes. 'No muscle. How's she going to handle them cows? Or chop wood?'

'She'll manage,' Mr Grace replies, leading the horse into the stable, 'if she knows what's good for her.'

'Well, she'd better.' A note of self-pity enters her voice. 'I'm still not right after bearing your child. I need help while I mend . . . You promised!'

Before I can pipe up to reassure her, Mr Grace storms from the stable and slams the door so hard it bounces back open again.

'Don't chide me, woman! You wanted a girl, so I've *got* you a girl. Now take her in hand and leave me in peace.'

Mrs Grace watches as he stomps off round the side of the house. She's muttering something and seems to have forgotten about me. I reach out to touch her shoulder . . . then think better of it. Her body almost hums with anger; puts me in mind of a wasps' nest. She spins round as I pick up my bag.

'Well? What's your name?'

'It's Annie,' I say, wondering how she's made that question sound like an accusation. 'Annie Mosey.'

Mrs Grace's face crumples as Eliza winds up and begins to howl. 'Oh no, not again . . .'

'Here, let me.' I take the baby, feeling her struggle inside the blanket. 'I think she just needs a bit of room.' Pleased with this chance to make a favourable impression, I head indoors . . . and stop on the threshold.

I'm in a large kitchen furnished with mismatched chairs and a table so badly stained I wonder if Mr Grace uses it to slaughter his hogs on. Dirty pots wallow in a sink of grey water. There's a tin bath by the pantry filled with sheets and soiled diapers. The floor's brown with trodden-in mud, the corners littered with mouse droppings. A doorway leads off into a dank corridor and some stairs leading up into darkness.

Ma always keeps our cabin clean and tidy no matter what, so this squalor shocks me. How could Mrs Grace let things get so bad? Then, as I watch her shuffle in behind me, looking lost inside her own home, I feel a wave of pity. She's been coping with a newborn pretty much on her own. Is it any wonder she's struggling? Well, I'm here now, and I can help get things back on track.

So. I lay Eliza on the table. Her eyes are screwed shut and she's bawling so loud there must be folk in Greenville wondering what the racket is. Mrs Grace lowers herself into a chair and presses the tips of her fingers to her forehead, but I see she's watching me.

'What a fuss,' I murmur to Eliza. 'Well, I think I know what's wrong . . .' I unwrap the blanket and am greeted by the ripest of baby smells. 'Phew! You *have* been busy.'

By the time I've washed and dressed her, Eliza's stopped crying and is gurgling away quite happily. 'I'm used to babies,' I say to Mrs Grace. 'I helped look after my sister, Huldie, before we had to give her away. I think Eliza just wanted to kick her legs about—'

The chair tips backwards with a clatter as Mrs Grace leaps up and snatches Eliza from my arms. 'I know what my child needs. I don't need *you* to tell me.'

I back away, frightened by this sudden switch in mood. 'I was just trying to help . . .'

'You're interfering.' She picks up the blanket and wraps Eliza up again. 'She must be kept warm. Don't you know that cold can kill a baby?'

'But it ain't cold in here—'

'It's cold enough.' She glares at me. 'I'd know.'

'I'm sorry . . .'

'I'm *sorry*, I'm *sorry*, I'm *sorry*. Well, we're all sorry for something.'

I'm actually pleased when Mr Grace appears at the door. 'Have you told her what she's here to do?'

'Not yet,' she says sullenly.

'Then for Christ's sake get her started on supper. It's been a long day and I'm hungry.'

I look at the dirty pots and dishes. I'll need to wash them all before I can even think about cooking. But right now, I just want some time on my own, a few minutes to catch my breath.

'Can I see my room first?'

'After supper,' he says. 'I'm going to feed the hogs and check 'em for fever. I expect it ready when I'm done.'

He stalks out, leaving me with no idea of how long I have, or what will happen if I'm late. Nothing good, *that's* for sure. Mrs Grace has disappeared somewhere with Eliza, so at least I'm on my own. Oh well, best foot forward, I suppose . . .

I find the larder, which is disorganised but well-stocked with packets, sacks and airtights, and throw together a stew of rabbit, potatoes, onions and pearl barley. By the time Mr Grace returns it's simmering away nicely on the stove. He surveys the tidier kitchen but makes no comment 'There's a crate of beer in the larder. Bring me two bottles.'

So, Mr Grace likes to pull a cork . . . I do as I'm told and he drains the first bottle in one go. He's just getting to work on the second when Mrs Grace shuffles in. Her dress is open and she's holding a wriggling Eliza against her naked breast. I look away, embarrassed.

'She won't suckle.' Mrs Grace looks close to tears. 'I know she's hungry, but she won't take anything. I don't know what I'm doing wrong . . .'

Mr Grace curls his lip. 'Cover yourself up, woman. The girl can give her some milk.'

Feeling even more sorry for Mrs Grace, I ladle some milk into a pan and set it on the stove. While it's warming, I fill three bowls with stew and hand them out. Mr Grace tucks in noisily. Mrs Grace just looks at it.

'Needs more salt,' he says with his mouth full. 'And the rabbit's tough. You didn't cook it long enough.'

'I cooked it for as long as I could,' I say with some heat.

He stops chewing and turns slowly towards me. 'Keep your tongue civil with me, girl, or you'll learn what happens.'

'Rabbit from that butcher's always tough,' Mrs Grace mutters. 'You should complain next time you're in town.'

'I can hunt,' I say hopefully. 'Whatever's in those woods out there, I'll bag it for you. If you lend me a gun I—'

'You won't touch my guns,' he says, 'and you won't go hunting. That's men's work.'

'But Mrs Edington said—'

'Never mind what she said.' He taps his chest with a beer bottle. 'From now on you heed *me*. And I say no shooting and no hunting, and no wandering about in the woods. Y'hear?'

I think about protesting, but only for a moment. Instead, I swallow my bitter disappointment and see to feeding Eliza. My stew's stone cold by the time she's finished, but I'm too tired to reheat it. I just force it down, congealed fat and all, and ask to see my room.

Mrs Grace leads me past a parlour and an office (where I catch a glimpse of a gunrack) on the ground floor, empty bedrooms upstairs, and up a ladder into the attic. There's a pillow and a pile of blankets on the floor – my 'bed', I guess – a chamber pot in the corner and a chair by a cracked window overlooking the hogs.

I turn to ask where the latrine is but she's already shuffling down the steps, leaving her candle behind. I close the trapdoor. Loneliness settles in my stomach, but I don't shed a tear. It won't help.

'Well, Annie,' I murmur. 'Let's make this place a bit homey.'

I fold the blankets to form a makeshift bed, sweep the worst of the mouse dropping and dust-balls into a corner, wipe the cobwebs and stack my clothes in the chest. My precious sewing kit, photograph and John's turkey I place on the windowsill. Then I put on my nightdress, clamber into bed and blow out the candle.

I'm about to doze off when I hear a screech from downstairs. It's her. She sounds furious, almost demented. Now he's joined in, a roar against her screams. I flinch at the sound of breaking glass and pull the blanket over my head.

21

'Wake up, girl.'

I emerge from a dark dream into a dark room and it takes me a moment to remember where I am. A shadow looms over me. Mr Grace.

'You awake?'

'Yu-yes.' I sit up, rubbing my eyes. 'What–?'

'It's time for work. Outside jobs. Get up.'

The ladder creaks as he clambers down. I sit upright and hug my knees. My back's stiff from the hard floorboards. Through the window black trees stand in front of a deep blue sky. Cold stars shine. Heck, it's not even sunrise. I crawl out of bed, get dressed and trudge downstairs. He's waiting for me in the lamplit kitchen.

I glance at the clock on the mantlepiece. It's five o'clock, a full hour earlier than I'd normally get up. 'What do you want me to do?' I yawn.

'To listen and remember. It's your job to make breakfast. Light the stove and put on the porridge and coffee. Then set out jam, butter, sugar and bread on the table.'

He stomps outside towards the cowshed. I follow. The cold helps to clear my sleep-addled brain.

'Cows want milking then herding to their field. Put the milk in the churn and don't spill any. You can give it to Eliza when Mrs Grace is having her trouble. The cows'll need hay from the feedstore twice a day when winter comes.' He points at the stable. 'Give Betsy a feedbag and a groom – and mind her teeth, she's a biter. There's a pitchfork and wheelbarrow for mucking out her stall. Take the manure to the heap round the back. And keep the water troughs full. Use the pump in the yard.'

We head round the side of the house and up to the hog pen. They trot over on dainty feet and point at us with flat, wet snouts.

'My hogs are always hungry,' Mr Grace says. 'They'll eat anything thrown in. Give them the kitchen scraps, rotten fruit and vegetables. I'm fattening them up for slaughter. Won't be long now.' And he's off again, skirting the fence towards the chicken coop. I have to run to keep up.

'Collect the eggs. Chickens need grain and fresh water.' He points to a tangle of bushes near the edge of the woods. 'Blackberries are in season. You can pick them and help Mrs Grace make jam. The kitchen garden's your responsibility. Needs sorting. When you've finished, keep it tidy and weeded. Anything rotten, give to the pigs. Tools are in that shed over there.'

I've to do all this as well as look after Eliza? I wonder what Mrs Grace'll be doing while I'm out here toiling. He's looking right at me in a way that makes my scalp crawl.

'Mrs Grace gets a lot of headaches,' he says. 'That's why you're here – to lighten her load and stop her nagging me all the time. Do that, and there'll be no trouble. Don't, and you'll learn what happens.' Mr Grace's threat ricochets around my mind as I set-to on my chores. He saddles Betsy around ten and heads into town – 'On business', he says – so I take the opportunity to have some breakfast, then it's back to work.

The sun reaches its zenith and I still ain't seen hide nor hair of Mrs Grace or Eliza. So, after cleaning myself up a bit and fixing a plate of eggs, I head up to her bedroom to check on them. There's no answer to my knock, so I go ahead and open the door. It's gloomy. The curtains are drawn. Eliza's kicking and fussing in her cot and Mrs Grace is in bed, facing away from me.

'Mrs Grace? Are you awake?' The blankets rustle as she stirs. 'Should I open the curtains for you?'

'No light.' Her voice sounds dull and lifeless. 'My head aches.'

'There's some eggs here for you . . .'

'Go away.'

'I'll just leave them here . . .' I try to put the plate on the bedside table but because it's so dark I miss and it crashes to the floor.

Mrs Grace sits up, half-tangling herself up in the bedcovers, and screams into my face. 'Get out! Get out! Getout-getout-get*out*!'

Shocked by her fury – I was only tryin' to help! – I grab Eliza and dash downstairs to the kitchen. After feeding her some warm milk and grabbing a bite to eat myself, I put her in a sling around my chest and head outside to finish my chores. Twilight's falling as I trudge back inside and find Mrs Grace sat sullenly at the table.

'Oh, mercy!' I exclaim when I see the cut across her nose and the purple bruise around her eye. 'What happened?'

But of course, I know. *He* did this to her. I may not like Mrs Grace, but no one deserves this. And what of Eliza? Growing up in a house with a man prone to such violence? And me . . . How long will it be before I end up on the wrong end of his fists?

'Never mind what happened,' Mrs Grace says. 'Have you finished your outside jobs?'

'Yes, but—'

'Then get on with supper. Mr Grace'll be back soon.'

'Nope. I ain't doin' nothing until I've washed that cut.'

She mumbles something then casts a hard glare at me with her one good eye. 'On *business*, is he?'

'That's what he said,' I say, pouring water from a kettle into a dish and casting round for a clean cloth. 'All right, just hold still . . .' Being as gentle as I can, I touch the wet cloth to the bridge of her nose. She screeches in pain and dashes the bowl to the floor with a vicious sweep of her arm.

'Clumsy wretch! I told you to get on with supper. If it ain't ready by the time he gets back he'll give you worse than this, believe me.' We both turn at the sound of an approaching horse. 'See what you've done?' Mrs Grace hisses.

I'm frightened, sure, but angry too. The kitchen darkens as Mr Grace appears in the doorway, and I know he's roostered the second I see his bloodshot eyes. He surveys Mrs Grace, the broken dish, then me.

'What's going on here?' His words slide into each other. 'Looks like idlin' to me.'

'I've not been idling,' I say through gritted teeth. 'I've not stopped all day.'

His protruding eyes widen. 'Then why ain't my supper ready? I won't be disobeyed . . . in my own house.'

'I told her,' Mrs Grace gabbles. 'I told her to get started ages ago but she don't listen.'

Mr Grace strides up so close he presses me back against the table. I smell the liquor on his breath. 'Consider this a warning. If you're late again with my supper I'll do to you what I did to her. Understand?'

My anger fizzles out. I nod my head and get on with supper.

22

I've only been here two weeks, but it already feels like years.

Every day is drudgery. I'm up before the sun and don't stop until long after it's set. *I* might do the cooking, but *he* dishes it up and never gives me enough. I reckon I'd have starved to death if I hadn't learned to sneak food: a slice of bread here, a handful of beans there. I guess I'm learning how to survive, get the better of them from time to time. But it's exhausting.

Eliza is the only source of light in this dark place. I take care of her most of the day. When she's not sleeping, I carry her against my chest in a sling, which keeps my arms free for work. It was a strain at first, but my back and shoulders are used to it now.

Of course *they* never help with anything, and are never grateful. *He* only deals with his precious hogs, and *she* spends most of her days in bed or moping around after me making nasty comments.

And if I make a mistake? Well . . .

The other day I dropped a pan of milk (my arms were tired after mucking out the cowshed) and Mrs Grace scuttled up and pinched me. Actually grabbed the fleshy part of my arm in her strong fingers and twisted until I squealed. She enjoyed it too. I nearly slapped her for that, but I knew that'd lead to far worse from *him*.

'*You're nothing,*' she said. '*You're trash. That's why your family threw you away.*'

I sometimes wonder if Mrs Grace has always been this way, or if it was her loveless marriage to a no-good drunk that dried up her heart and soured her soul.

My only respite is at the end of the day when I retreat to the attic. Sometimes I sit by the window and imagine escaping this place with Eliza. I could follow the road to town and catch the train to Greenville . . . But I can't do that. What would Mrs Edington say if I ran away? She'd think me weak and disobedient, and send me straight back. Besides, there's the money to consider.

Yesterday they sat me down to write a letter home. Well, *she* wrote it and in the end it was mostly her words, not mine.

Do not worry about me. I am doing well on the farm. I work hard but the Graces are kind. I am very happy here, especially when exploring the woods and learning to ride Betsy the horse.

All lies, of course. But the Graces know – as do I – that if Ma discovered the truth she'd come straight here and fetch me home. They can't have that because they'd lose their slave. And *I* can't have that because then Ma wouldn't get the money that Mr Grace puts in the envelope along with the letter.

I want to explore the woods, maybe even lay a few traps. If I'm lucky, I might find a secret place to build a fire so I can cook what I catch and eat it all my darn self. Anything to get one over on the Graces.

So, while he's off buying hog feed and she and Eliza are asleep upstairs, I've been working extra-fast to get my chores done early. I'm finished now and I reckon I've got a couple of precious hours to myself before anyone misses me.

I'm halfway across the yard when I hear the front door open. 'Where do you think *you're* going, trash?' My heart sinks. I turn. There she is, glaring at me with those button-hard eyes of hers.

My disappointment hardens to resentment. Can't she leave me alone for five minutes? 'I've finished all my chores. I just want to go for a walk—'

'A walk?' she snaps. 'You're here to work, not walk.'

She smiles a nasty smile, goes indoors for a moment then reappears, tucking something into her pocket. 'Come with me.'

I follow her to the latrine – a crooked, windowless little

shack behind the house. Inside is a seat with a hole where we do our business into a pit. It's filthy and stinks to high heaven (especially on hot days like today) and I always get in and out as fast as I can.

'I want this scrubbed so it shines,' she says. 'That'll mend your idle ways.'

I bite down on my words, rigid with anger. There's something else this time, an extra pinch of cruelty in her face. She takes an envelope from her pocket and holds it up.

'Mr Grace picked this up from town the other day. It's a letter. For you. From your ma, probably.'

A letter! A precious link to home . . . I hold out my hand just as a sickening realisation hits me: she's not going to hand it over without first getting her pound of flesh. I withdraw my hand and wait.

'Clean the latrine well enough and you can have this,' she says. 'I'll even read it to you. I know you've not had the instruction to do so on your own.'

I glare at her, but I know I can't do anything 'cept obey. I fetch water, cloths, a broom. I sweep out hundreds of dead flies and pour cleansing lime – a white powder that makes my skin itch – into the pit. Then, with a cloth wrapped around my mouth, I get on my hands and knees and scrub the floor and walls with soapy water until my hands are raw and my arms are shaking. And all the while she watches with a smile twitching around her lips.

It's funny though. When I finish and step back to look at the glistening wooden boards, I feel quite pleased with myself. I bet it wasn't this clean when it was first built!

'There,' I say. 'All done. Can I have my letter now?'

I know right away from the look in her eye that she was never going to give me the letter. She just steps around me, drops it into the pit and heads back to the farmhouse.

23

SPRING 1871

After a long winter, the world is coming back to life. There's sticky buds forming on the trees and flowers poking through the grass. I guess it cheers me up a bit. At least I won't be so darn cold at night. The Graces aren't awake yet and I'm in my favourite spot, a dip in the pasture that can't be seen from the house. While I savour this rare moment of peace, Eliza's enjoying her most favourite pastime of crawling around on the grass and laughing at Lord knows what.

Mr Grace tossed a letter to me last night and I had to beg Mrs Grace to read it to me (and don't I wish I'd listened to Mary Jane when she'd tried to teach me all those times!). Eventually she agreed, but she spoke it in a foolish, mocking tone. Don't matter. When I look at Ma's neat handwriting I can make out just enough of the words to remind me of the whole thing.

I reckon Ma's written lots of times, but Mr Grace doesn't always bother to pick the letters up, or he just keeps them from me to be cruel. I write home every two weeks (under *their* supervision, of course) and Mr Grace slips the precious two dollars into the envelope.

I unfold the letter and carefully work my way along the lines . . .

Dear Annie,

I hope this finds you well. I can't tell you how happy I am that you've found a good home with the Graces. I am certain you are growing up to be a fine young woman.

I have tidings. First, Lydia is courting. Farm business takes her into Greenville fairly often these days, and it was whilst there that she met her new beau, a Mr Joseph Stein. I judge him to be quite respectable, and he earns a decent living as a building supplier in Cincinnati. He visits us often despite the long journey, which I take as a sign of his honest affection. Lydia is being uncharacteristically cautious, and I suspect she's inhibiting herself from making plans that take her away from the farm because it will make things even more difficult for we who remain. For myself, I wish her to fly to wherever happiness waits for her.

Which brings me to my other slice of news. I am to marry again. My husband-to-be is an honest, hardworking man from Woodland whom I have known as a friend for many years. Be assured that our affection for each other is quite genuine, but I also judge that the help and strength he'll provide around the farm will both keep the roof over our heads and afford Lydia the freedom to pursue her own destiny with Mr Stein. I pray that is the outcome, anyway.

I still love your dear departed Pa, but I cannot live the rest of my life alone. I hope you'll find it in your warm and generous heart to be happy for me.

With love,
Ma

I mull over her words, as I did all last night. It sure sounds like things are tough, despite the money Mr Grace sends. And regarding Ma's news, on the one hand I'm glad that some good things are happening to those I hold most dear. On the other, everything at home is changing and I'm not there to be part of it. That makes me lonesome, and I wonder if there'll there be a place for me back home, if ever I get to leave this place?

24

FALL 1871

Having been in this miserable place for a year, I've learned to find light and pleasure in the smallest of things: Eliza's laugh, a stolen walk in the forest, even pulling faces behind the Graces' backs. Today it's this: my first potato harvest.

It's taken me ages, but I've turned what was an overgrown mess into a flourishing kitchen garden full of herbs, turnips, onions, pumpkins and beans. Digging, planting, weeding, watering, running around and flapping my arms to scare the birds away . . . It's been hard work, but this place is now my pride and joy.

I thrust my hands into the soil and have a feel around. I find a potato, but it squishes to mush. Oh well, there are always a few spoiled in a crop . . . I dig around and find a bigger one. Seems firm enough. I work it up through the dirt.

My heart sinks. Half is soft, grey and inedible. I find another. It collapses into paste. As the first queasy pangs of panic slither into my stomach, I yank more out by their stems and before I know it, I'm surrounded by uprooted plants, churned-up earth and a scattering of rotten potatoes. I'm so distracted I don't notice Mr Grace until he speaks.

'Looks like Gettysburg.' He picks up a spoiled potato. 'They all blighted?'

I nod, feeling wretched.

'You left the harvest too late. Should have dug 'em up sooner. I'll have to go into town now and buy some.'

'I'm sorry, I didn't know about—'

'That's time and money you've cost me.'

I look around to see if there's more plants I've not checked . . . Then something hard smacks me in the forehead. I stagger backwards, catch my foot in a hole and land on my rump. I wipe my face and my hand comes away covered in pulped potato.

I scramble to my feet, burning with a desire to retaliate. I've a potato in my hand so I hurl it. Mr Grace jerks to one side with a delicious look of surprise on his face. The potato glances off his shoulder, leaving a slimy smear behind. He swipes it away then lunges towards me.

I dodge from his first grab but stumble on a loose bit of turf. He grasps me by the elbow and yanks me so hard my arm nearly pops from its socket. 'Let go,' I gasp. 'You're *hurting* me!'

'Time to teach you a lesson.'

He drags me around the side of the house and onto the porch. One of my boots slides off. '*Letgo, letgo, letgo!*' I grab the doorframe with one hand, but it's no use. One tug and my grip's ripped loose. We're in the kitchen, the corridor, and finally the worst room in the house: the back room. It's cold and full of broken shadows. Mould blossoms on damp walls. Rats scurry in the shadows. I *never* come in here.

Mr Grace stops in front of an empty wardrobe and shoves me inside so hard, I smack my forehead on the opposite wall. Then he slams the door and locks it. Darkness swallows me; panic, hot and thick as molasses, fills my throat. I hurl myself at the door, hammering, thumping and kicking – but it hardly even moves.

Bruised, quaking, and feeling an almighty throb building in my temple, I peer through the keyhole just in time to see Mr Grace leave the room. He must have waited so he could listen to my cries . . . and in that moment rage sets fire to my heart and limbs.

Bracing my shoulders against the back wall, I place my feet against the door, grit my teeth and push, push, *push* . . . but it's too strong and all it does is creak.

Eventually, drained of strength, I curl up on the floor to wait in the cold and listen to the rats scuttle under the floorboards.

Time drags. The urge to visit the latrine comes and goes in increasingly desperate waves. I hum to myself to take my mind off that, the loneliness, and the painful bruises on my shins, forehead and hands. Just like Red Riding Hood, I'm alone in the woods and far from home – 'cept I'm fighting against *two* Big Bad Wolves and there ain't no hunter coming to rescue me.

The Wolves. That's who they are to me now.

It's dark when Mr Wolf opens the door and stalks off without a word. I uncurl myself and have to shake out my cramped legs before I can make the dash to the latrine – and I'm only just in time. I stay on the seat, even after my bladder's emptied, shaking with shame that I know I don't deserve.

He locked me up and left me for hours, and there ain't nothing to stop him from doing it again. He might even leave me longer next time, and the thought of stewing in my own filth is too humiliating to bear. I need a plan . . .

My mind whirls as I at last emerge into the cool evening air. The wardrobe's big – wider than its doors. That means there's room to stash things out of sight. What if I put a blanket in there? A candle and some matches? A bucket for latrine emergencies? Such things would make the imprisonment a mite more bearable. I feel a tiny bit better when I resolve to carry out my plan. Any victory over him, no matter how small, is worth savouring.

25

SPRING 1872

The bread's baked, the butter's been churned and the kitchen floor's scrubbed as well as I can manage (it always looks kinda dirty though). So, my morning jobs are done, and the best part is Mr Wolf's out and about somewhere and Mrs Wolf's in bed with one of her headaches (Eliza's sleeping too) – and that means a bit of time to myself.

I'm just heading towards the stairs to go up to my room when I notice the door to Mr Wolf's office, which he usually keeps locked, is standing ajar. I approach, knowing that if Mr Wolf catches me he'll probably throw me in the wardrobe again.

Taking a moment to ensure my enemies definitely aren't around, I creep into the office. It's a poky little room with a desk, a rusty stove and a cloying smell of tobacco in the air; one of the desk drawers is open and I see, tucked at the back, a jar filled with dollar bills.

But I don't care about that – my eyes are drawn to the gun rack. He's got a Winchester repeater, a Springfield rifle and two double-barrelled shotguns. Well-oiled and clean, seems they're about the only things in his life he *does* look after. Sunlight from the window gleams on their polished stocks.

Oh, what I wouldn't give to take that Winchester into the forest, bag me a grouse, cook it over a fire and eat it all myself!

Thing is, these guns are wasted on Mr Wolf. I could outhunt him *any* day of the week. I've watched him blundering through the undergrowth with his rifle, scaring all the game away. He hardly ever brings anything back; most of the meat they eat (I never get a morsel) he buys from the butcher.

I run my fingers along one of the shotgun barrels, itching to pick it up, see how it feels . . . I poke my head into the hallway, listen carefully, then close the door.

I lift the shotgun from its wooden cradle. It's heavy, solid, balanced. The metal is cool and ever-so-slightly oily under my fingers. I thumb a lever on the side and the barrel drops smoothly on a hinge, exposing the two breeches where the cartridges are loaded. I snap it closed (so satisfying!), plant the stock into my shoulder and sight down the barrels. I wonder how long I can keep it steady?

I turn at the sound of approaching bootsteps, slow and heavy. It's him! I feel faint, like all the blood's drained out through my soles. I lunge for the gunrack and bump my hip against the desk corner; the shotgun slips from my grasp and clatters to the floor. Knowing he must only be a few paces from the door, I pick up the gun and fumble it back into place.

I spin round as the door opens and stand rigidly in front

of the gunrack. I try to look calm, but my face feels flushed. He stops in the doorway, smelling of hog. I know I look guilty. I know I look afraid. Oh God, please don't let him notice . . .

'What are you doing in here?'

I try to make my voice sound light. 'I was about to sweep the floor.'

'Why was the door closed?'

'I didn't want to disturb Mrs Grace.' I point to the ceiling. 'She's in bed with a headache.'

He looms over me. 'You're not allowed in here. I told you that.'

'I forgot.' I lean back, gripping the desktop. 'I wanted to sweep everywhere . . .'

He slowly surveys the room then pins his gaze back on me. Something squirms in my guts. 'So. Where's your broom?'

'I . . . I don't know. I must have forgotten it.'

'Something else you've forgotten.'

'Yes,' I say, making for the doorway. 'I'll go fetch it . . .'

He shuts the door with a kick of his heel. 'You've been messing with my guns.'

'No, I've not.' My voice is nothing but a whisper.

'I told you never to touch them.'

His voice and expression haven't changed. He doesn't seem angry, yet I know I'm in more trouble than I've ever been before. My stomach's a grinding knot. My legs feel like they've been deboned.

'Please, I'm sorry. I'll go to my room—'

In one smooth motion he twists at the waist, raises his arm – there's a moist scab on his elbow – and strikes my face with the back of his hand. I'm suddenly on the floor. For a moment I can't move for shock, then I scramble under the desk and cower with a hand pressed against my burning face. Blood trickles between my fingers. He's torn my cheek with his ring.

'Come out from there.'

'No. Leave me alone!'

'You disobeyed me. Then you lied.'

Wood screeches against wood as he heaves the desk away, leaving me exposed. He grips my neck and drags me to my feet. I kick, scream and wriggle, but he just holds me at arm's length until I go limp as a throttled rabbit.

'Let go,' I gasp. 'I . . . can't . . . breathe . . .'

He tightens his fingers. Black dots swirl in front of my eyes.

'I'm going to beat the sneakiness out of you,' he says, spinning me around and shoving me up against the desk. There's a hiss as he slides the belt from his pants and a creak of leather as he wraps the end around his fist.

'Please don't . . .'

'Put your hands on the desk. If you move, or fall over, I'm starting again.'

I grip the desk and squeeze my eyes shut.

*

I'm in bed, lying on my front. Stripes of pain run from my shoulders to the bottom of my spine, over my behind, and down to the back of my knees. Some sting, like I've been whipped with nettles, others are raw from where the belt buckle's bitten skin. I can't see what damage he's done, and even if I had a mirror I'd be too frightened to look. I can see my dress though. It's ripped, bloodied, and lying on the floor where I left it.

From the moment I arrived at this place I've been miserable and lonely – but when they starve me I sneak food, and when they leave me in the wardrobe I huddle in my blanket and wait them out. What can I do against a beating as savage as that? I'm just a child, small for my age and with no one to turn to.

I could leave. Make off in the night. But could Ma get by without the money Mr Wolf sends? Would she be able to feed everyone? Pay the mortgage? Probably not. She never says outright in her letters, but I get the impression times are still hard and there's a chance the family might end up at the Infirmary. And if *that* happens, they might be split up and sent to live with strangers. Imagine little John in a hellhole like this . . .

No. I won't risk that. I'm staying. But to survive I've got to be more careful. I must be cunning. Wily. A fox against two wolves.

26

SUMMER 1872

The blackberries are out early this year, so I'm up by the woods to fill a basket. My fingers are black with juice, and I'm eating more than I'm harvesting. They're delicious! Eliza's toddling about by a fragrant patch of wild mint. A light breeze, full of summer warmth, rustles the leaves and entices me into the trees. As usual, I can't resist.

A quick glance tells me the enemy's nowhere in sight, so I pick Eliza up, hop over the fence and venture into the wood's cool shadow. Feeling the soft loam under my feet and hearing the birds in the branches is a salve on my soul. The stiffness in my limbs earned from my daily grind and the bruises from my latest hiding recede a little as I creep further away from the farm and the beasts, savage as meat axes, who live there.

'Look there, Eliza,' I murmur. 'That's an oak tree. And up there – a squirrel! See? Looks mischievous, don't he? I bet he's up to some monkeyshines.'

Deeper we go, my spirits rising with every step. I escape here fairly often, but only when it's safe. I haven't dug any traps because I can never predict when I'll be able to come and check them, and I don't want some poor ground bird falling in and starving to death 'cos I'm stuck on the farm under *their* beady eyes.

I sometimes try to imagine what the Wolves were like when they first married. More confounding is why they did so in the first place, cos there ain't no love between 'em. Far from it – if anything, they seem to *hate* each other. They bicker and fight constantly, and he beats her nearly as often as he does me. The scale of his belligerence is matched only by her misery – until he gets slewed and becomes even worse.

I'm surviving by forming a kind of shell around myself. I pay my attention to Eliza and the animals; I never speak to or spend time with *them* unless I absolutely have to. I do my work without complaint, take my little victories (like this jaunt into the trees) whenever I can, and never go anywhere without John's wooden turkey – my good luck charm – in my pocket.

I often think of the cabin, my family, what they're up to, what they're spending their regular two dollars on, and praying that they're safe and sound. But these thoughts have a price, because they come with real pain, a sense of time slipping by being out of their company, away from their warmth and love, and of precious moments and memories that should have been, but never were. I push the thoughts down deep, add another layer to my shell, and head back – regretfully, sadly – to the farm.

27

WINTER 1872

This hardly ever happens, but I've actually got some time to myself. *He's* in town on business and won't be back until tomorrow and *she's* gone to bed with Eliza. So tonight I'm sitting in front of the parlour fire with nothing to do but mend one of Eliza's blankets.

It's the middle of my third winter here, and it's one of the worst I've encountered. Snow ain't let up for days, and the cold seeped into this big old house weeks ago and hasn't left. I stretch my legs out and let the heat lick my bare feet. After endless days working outdoors and sleepless nights shivering under my blankets, it's heaven to be warm. The orange glow even softens the dirty-blue bruises on my arms.

My fingers are getting tired, so I put my darning on my lap to give them a rest. I run my hands up my arms and across my shoulders, feeling the hard muscle. I'm twelve now, still quite short and dead skinny, but tougher in mind and body than I was when I got here, that's for sure.

Goodness, but my eyes are getting heavy! A full stomach

and a fire are making me drowsy . . . Perhaps I'll close them, just for a moment . . .

'Just what do you think you're doing, trash?'

I open my eyes and gasp. Mrs Wolf's snarling face fills my sight. Her hair is awry and there's a vein pulsing in her neck. She snatches the darning from my lap and shakes it under my nose.

'You were supposed to finish this! Do you want my child to freeze to death?' She grabs my wrist and yanks me to my feet. 'That's not your chair. That's *my* chair. Lazy little wretch!'

After over two years of living with her moods, I know this tantrum is nothing but a sham, an act to frighten me. I see the glee in her eyes. She's delighted I've given her an excuse to dish out another punishment. My only revenge is to pretend I don't care. I fold my arms and fire her a sullen look.

Her face twists with real anger and she draws back a shaking fist. I start to raise my hands but I'm too slow. Sharp knuckles strike my brow. I stumble backwards, only to be struck again. Pain splits my thoughts. Bloodspots patter onto the floorboards. My left eye feels mushy. I look up. She's just a crooked, screaming shape.

Mrs Wolf's never punched me before. She usually pinches, slaps and twists – cruel little squalls I weather and turn my back on. I shake my head to clear it and see her arm's cocked and her hand's still a white-knuckled fist. She's fixing to hit me again.

'Nooo!'

It's part word, part howl. Rage bursts from where I've kept it deep inside. It pours into my muscles, unleashing strength I never knew I had. I spring forward and shove her in the chest. She falls backwards, cracks her head against the floor and goes still.

Stunned? Dead? In this moment, lost amid my fury, *I just don't care.*

I bend over her to see. Her eyes snap open and she grabs a fistful of my hair. Scalding pain envelops my scalp as she gets up and drags me across the floor. Biting down on a scream, I reach behind to prise open her grip, but her claws are buried deep.

'You'll pay,' she pants. 'Just wait!'

'Let *go* of me!'

Mrs Wolf throws open the door, letting in a blast of freezing air. I wriggle, trying to shake her loose, but she's too strong, too wrathful. Iron fingers curl around my ankle and she half-lifts me from the floor.

'I'll let go all right!' she says and throws me outside.

Gasping in pain but still *raging*, I get to my feet and lunge for the door. She's on the threshold, a silhouette against the kitchen glow, and with a swing of her arm slams the door in my face.

'You can stay out there til you freeze to death,' she shouts, sliding the bolts across. 'No one'll miss you. And if you try to come back in, I'll douse your lights with a carving knife.'

I step back from the door. My fury leaks away, leaving nothing behind but dread. I wrap my arms around my chest. The cold's already bitten through my dress. My breath turns into swirling clouds. I look at my bare feet and see they're already as white as the snow they're half-buried in.

What if I open a window and sneak back inside? Would she really try to kill me? *Yes, tonight, I believe she would.* My skin is stiff with gooseflesh, I can hardly feel my toes and fingers, and I have to clench my jaw to stop my teeth chattering.

'*Rurr, rurr, rurr...*'

I trudge away from the house, sure only of one thing: I won't give her the satisfaction of seeing me shivering and turning blue. I make my way through the snow to the cowshed and try to lift the iron bar across the doors, but the ice has frozen it solid and there's no way, in my increasingly weakening state, that I'll be able to open it. I try the stables and smokehouse too, all to no avail.

I slip into the gap between the stable wall and the woods, hoping it'll afford me some shelter. How has this happened? A moment ago I was dozing by the fire. Now I'm trapped outside in the cold. I think of Pa, turned almost to ice, his blackened fingers bent into hooks that never opened again. That could happen to *me* . . .

'*Rurr, rurr, rurr...*'

I imagine the morning sun casting its light onto a little mound of snow. Beneath the mound is me, curled up like a sleeping cat with balls of ice in my eye sockets. No, no, *no* . . .

I drop to my knees and clasp my fingers together. My lips are too cold to speak, so I say a prayer in my mind asking God to forgive my sins, and not let me die in the cold. I look up to the heavens. Snowflakes still spiral but most of the clouds have gone, leaving behind a haloed moon in a black sky. I stare deep and long, until my vision goes blurry. Just what is it I'm hoping to see in those teeming stars? God's bearded face? Jesus, smiling? Pa? Mary Jane?

I don't know. Perhaps just a sign that someone's listening, knows how much I'm suffering, and how hard I'm trying to survive.

'Hu-help me,' I manage. 'Puh-please. Amen.'

The cold's right through to my bones. I'm not just shivering any more, I'm quaking, juddering, *tremoring*.

'*Rurr, rurr, rurr . . . Rurr, rurr, rurr . . .*'

I rub my hands up and down my arms. Rock back and forth on my haunches. Hunch my shoulders. Press my chin into my chest. Try to capture my thoughts.

Did Pa pray when he was freezing?

My fingers feel warm, but I can't bend them.

If I die, will the Wolves tell anyone?

I'm sitting by Pa's bedside, holding his dear hand.

Head's a dead weight. Turned to solid bone.

Hoping that he'll give me a sign.

Will they bury me in the woods?

Breathing slow. Little puffs of fog.

Oh, the joy I felt when he squeezed my fingers!

No, they'll feed me to the pigs.

I shall lean against the stable.

Just for a moment.

And close my eyes.

'Rurr, rurr, rurr . . .'

A *thump*. In my back. Another. Hard enough to make the wall shake.

'Whaa . . . ?'

I press a hand to the frost-rimed wood. *Thump. Judder.* The wall's rattling! A rusty nail pings from its hole. *Thump. Judder.* Then Betsy neighing. She's kicking her stall wall, right by where I'm kneeling.

Does she know I'm here?

I drag myself up and work my way around the stable until I reach the closed half-doors. I have to get inside – if I don't, I'm sure to die. Once again I try the top bolt, but it's still stiff with ice, my fingers feel like rubber and I just can't get a grip. But this time I don't give up and, spurred on by Betsy's kicks, I look around for something I can use as a lever.

I find a stick, wedge it under the bolt handle, lever it up then wiggle it across. The top door creaks open. I clamber over and close it behind me. It's still freezing inside, but at least it's out of the wind. Betsy's looking at me from her stall. She shakes her head and whinnies.

'Wu-why are you making su-such a racket, eh, Bu-betsy?' I wrap my arms around her neck and press my face into her mane. 'Tu-trying to wu-wake me up?'

Hay rustles as she shuffles her hooves. Using a stool, I clamber onto her back then wriggle, stomach down, under the blanket. I rub my arms against her flanks and bury my face into her mane. I don't know how long it takes, but her warmth slowly seeps into me and I believe I'll survive the night. And there's something else I've come to realise. Something that changes everything.

Mrs Wolf doesn't care if I die. Mrs Wolf nearly killed me.

Calm falls over me as I make a decision. I'm going to escape. Tomorrow. Before Mr Wolf returns.

28

Betsy stood patiently all night as I drifted in and out of sleep. Bouts of shivering took hold of me as the hours before daylight dragged by.

I slip to the ground when the dawn sun shines through the cracks in the walls and crouch on the floor to gather my strength. My head's heavy, my thoughts slow. Feels like my brains have frozen.

The cold bites straightaway, so I wrap the blanket around my shoulders and hop from one bare foot to the other. Icicles hang from the ceiling, the walls are white with frost, and my and Betsy's breath comes out as fog. I creep to the door, rubbing some life into my arms, and peek outside.

All's quiet and covered in snow so bright it hurts my eyes. There's the forest track leading away from this place – this place that nearly became my grave. In the other direction lies the house and Mrs Wolf. I must hurry.

'You saved me last night, Betsy,' I say as I stroke her neck. 'Thank you. Now I need your help again. You fancy a ride into town?' She snorts and gives me a gentle head-bump.

I put the blanket over her back and attach the reins. I ain't strong enough to lift the saddle so I'll have to ride bareback, but I reckon I've had enough practice on Maple to make the trip.

I need to get indoors, but the front door's locked and it might be hours before *she* ventures outside. So I grab a hammer and chisel from a tool rack and open the stable door.

'All right, Betsy,' I whisper, 'wait here till I get back.'

Then I'm off towards the house, heart pounding and ready for the fight. I skirt around the edge til I reach his workshop window. It's frozen up, so I get to work with the hammer and chisel, tap-tap-tapping and chip-chip-chipping the ice away around the whole frame. Every noise shreds my already tattered nerves, but all I can do is pray neither Mrs Wolf nor Eliza hears it and wakes up.

I work as fast as I can, as the cold seeps into my flesh and it gets harder to hold the tools. Once done, I wedge the chisel into a gap at the bottom and lever the window open (wincing at every scrape and squeal) just far enough for me to slip through.

I take a few dollars from the money jar then poke my head out the door. All I hear is a steady drip of water from the pump in the kitchen. Good. *She* must still be in bed, utterly uncaring of my deadly plight in the cold. Wishing my teeth would stop chattering, I dash up to my room, put on my warmest clothes then wrap the precious photograph, thread box and turkey in a blanket and put them in my bag.

I'm ready, and all I need do is slip out the front door, mount Betsy and get the heck out of here. Then it's into town, onto a train and home to Greenville. I stop at the top of the ladder. At the bottom, on the right, is *her* room. A sudden fear grips me. What if she's awake? What if she's hiding in the shadows with a knife, waiting to make good on her promise to 'douse my lights'?

I close my eyes and whisper, 'Please, God, give me the courage I need. Amen,' then make my way down to the landing. I pause outside her door. Dear Eliza'll be in there too, and I'm filled with the urge to creep in and take her with me, rescue her from the Wolves and this lonely, loveless farm.

But I can't. She's not my child, and they'd soon track me down and take her back. Besides, they're not cruel to her like they are to me. All I can do is pray that she don't end up like them. I press my hand against the door as a token goodbye . . . then a thump like a footstep from inside the bedroom sets my heart pounding anew.

All thoughts of quiet fly like panicked birds and I pound down those stairs just as fast as I can. I'm halfway down when I hear the bedroom door open, and I can't help but look . . . She's at the top, wild hair framing a wild face. She lets out a howl and throws herself down the stairs after me.

I take the rest in one leap. My boots clatter as I sprint to the front door. I fumble at the bolts, drawing them back, knowing she's only seconds behind me with her grasping hands. I throw open the door, dash through and pull it shut – just as she reaches it. I keep a-hold of the handle, feet slipping on the porch as she tries to yank it open from the inside. I scream every time it opens and I catch a glimpse of bared teeth and a staring eye.

Terrified and weakened, my grip on the handle slips. I glance over at the stable – it looks a long way off – count to three and set off running towards it. The door bangs open behind me.

'Running away, s'that it?' she shrieks. 'Well, you won't get far!'

By the time I skid into the stable my breath's coming in long, ragged gasps. I untie Betsy, clamber onto her back with my bag and take the reins. Where's Mrs Wolf? She could only have been a few paces behind me . . . Gripping Betsy's flanks between my thighs, I urge her forward with a kick of my heels, ducking sideways as she trots through the door. I glance towards the house.

She's only halfway across the yard! Stumbling on the ice in nothing but her bare feet!

'Get off that horse, trash!' she yells. 'You get off right now, or I'll beat you blind.'

Betsy gives an uneasy whinny, slows down and half-turns

towards Mrs Wolf. I pat her neck, say 'Walk on', and off she trots towards the track again.

'Get *back* here, you vicious little wretch!' Her voice is further away, and there's more desperation in it than anger. 'Oh, I'll fix you proper *this* time!'

I glance behind. She's still hobbling after me, leaving pink footprints in the snow. I draw Betsy to a stop at the track entrance. A breeze plucks at my hair as I wait. When she's only a few paces away I nudge with my heel and off we go again.

'No, don't you *dare*!'

On she hobbles, her face and footprints getting ever-redder. I let her catch up again, wait until she's reaching out, then set Betsy on her way. I look round just in time to see Mrs Wolf trip and fall flat on her face. I turn away and don't look back until I'm out of the forest.

All I need to do is follow the road. If I see Mr Wolf returning home, I'm going to steer Betsy into the trees and hope he doesn't spot me. And if he does, I'll ride away as fast as I can. He's not getting his hands on me again without a fight. No, sir.

I just hope I'm really going in the right direction . . . there's trees blocking my view on both sides, so I've got no landmarks to head towards. After an hour of uncertain riding, the woods thin out. Traffic – carts, riders and people – join me on the road and I see a busy little town ahead. Sweet relief fills me and I bend down to give Betsy a stroke.

She doesn't seem to mind the milling people, trotting horses and rattling carts, and she works her way through the throng with hardly any cajoling from me. I can see the train station – a long building with smoke rising from behind it. A train's in. I wonder if it's bound for Greenville?

There's a wagon ahead, rolling towards me through the crowd. I don't know the driver, but I recognise his companion instantly, and my heart climbs into my throat. It's Mr Wolf, hunched over, looking sullen. Probably hungover after a night's drinking with his buddy. I glance around for an escape route – a side street or alley – but there are none. Besides, I'm hemmed in by the traffic. I could dismount and run, but that might catch his attention.

No. I've got to brazen it out. I give my head a little shake so my hair hangs over my face, but I resist the urge to speed up, hunch down in my seat or turn away. He's going to pass by my left side, close enough to reach out and grab me. Twenty paces, ten . . . His wagon jolts and I see him mouth a curse.

We draw level. I'm gripping the reins so tight my fingernails dig into my palms. I glimpse his bristly hands, a mud stain on his jacket and then he's gone. I stare ahead and don't turn round until I reach the train station. Quivering with relief, I slip from Betsy's back and tie her to a hitching post.

'Thank you,' I say, pressing my cheek against her head. 'I'd never have got away without you. And don't worry, I'll make sure someone comes and collects you.'

With a final goodbye pat, I enter the station, march up to the ticket booth and ask the agent inside for my ticket to freedom.

After a couple of hours and several stops at smaller burgs, the train grinds to a halt in Greenville station. On any other occasion I'd have been thrilled by such a novel experience – the rattling carriages, the bridges over rivers, the farms and woodlands rolling past – but recent events are still hanging over me like thunderclouds, and I don't feel safe yet.

I pick up my bag and step down onto the crowded platform. So many people! So much noise! Conversating, shouting greetings, clattering about with their trunks, travelling cases and hatboxes. Behind me the steam engine puffs and blows like a winded ox.

I pick my way through the station building, feeling like a stranger in a new land. A handsome couple in fine and fancy togs are buying tickets for Cincinnati. A man in a stovepipe hat says something to his companions and they all burst out laughing. A little girl dashes onto the platform chased by her mother. 'Estelle!' she cries. 'I told you not to run away.'

Run away. *Run away.* That's what I've gone and done. Escaped and left the Wolves to their darkness.

A young man tips his bowler and opens the station door for me. 'Afternoon, Miss. Fine day, ain't it?'

I stare at him. Such courtesy seems strange after two years of cruelty and it takes me a moment to muster a response. 'Good afternoon, sir,' I eventually say. 'It sure is.'

Main Street's busy and I have to make my way through the crowd. Feels like wading upstream. Past the barbershop, the drugstore, the big white church. There's a brewery smell in the air: malt and hops. A doorbell tinkles from a nearby shop.

These sights, sounds and smells are familiar from my life before, yet now I feel separate from it all. Everything's the same . . . 'cept me. I glance over my shoulder, half-expecting to see Mr Wolf barging through the crowd towards me.

Grab that girl! She's mine!

He's not there. Course he ain't. He's *miles* away, probably giving hell to Mrs Wolf for letting me escape, but still my heart pounds crazily and my breath comes in painful gasps.

I must get to the Infirmary. I'll only be safe behind that big door. I step into the road and run, run, run nearly as fast as the questions a-whirling through my mind. How am I going to explain about everything? What if they don't believe me? *What if they send me back?*

I stop at the Infirmary gate, catch my breath then walk up the path and knock on the door. Footsteps approach from inside and relief washes over me like warm water when Mrs

Edington opens the door. For a moment she looks at me without a flicker of recognition, then her eyes widen.

'Annie?' she says, crouching down and taking hold of my hands. 'My Lord, but there's nothing *of* you . . . And your face . . . Oh, my dear, whatever's happened to you?'

'I've been away,' I whisper, and throw my arms around her neck.

29

Mrs Edington watches with a curled forefinger pressed against her lips as I sit at a refectory table wolfing down stew and cornbread. It's the best meal I've had for I don't know how long. I'm just about finished when a resident comes in and whispers, 'Bath's ready,' to Mrs Edington.

'Thank you,' she replies. 'Right then, Annie. Let's get you cleaned up.'

I stand . . . too quickly, because everything goes blurry and I have to grab the table to stop myself falling. Mrs Edington scoops me up. 'Dear Lord,' she mutters, 'you're light as a feather.'

She carries me into a bathroom full of steam and soapy smells and sets me gently down on the floor. 'There, this will do you the world of good. Arms up, dear . . .' She lifts the dress over my head. 'Oh, Annie!' she gasps. 'Just what have you endured? Scars and bruises . . . all down your poor back . . .'

'They're from Mr Wolf,' I whisper.

'Mr Wolf?' Her voice trembles. 'You mean Mr Grace?'

I shake my head. Memories flood my mind. The crack of his belt, the tears and pain that followed. I'm shaking, but I don't let myself cry. I won't waste another drop on *him*. I turn round, arms stiff at my sides. My voice sounds dull in my ears. 'I escaped, and I won't go back.'

'You're not going anywhere,' Mrs Edington says. 'You're staying right here with us.' My shoulders drop and I let out a long breath. 'Now go on, into the bath with you.'

I finish undressing and slip all the way under the water. My cuts and bruises burn for a moment before the heat cocoons me. All sound retreats, my hair floats free around my head. I open my eyes, see ripples of dancing light, and feel safe for the first time in two years.

Rurr, rurr, rurr . . . Rurr, rurr, rurr . . .

Cold. So *cold* . . .

Can't stop shivering.

Where . . . ?

On my side. Curled in a ball. Eye's throbbing. Feels too big for its socket. Am I still with *them*? Was my escape just a dream?

Open your eyes. Be brave and open them . . .

It's dark but I see meadow flowers and bluebirds. It's wallpaper. I feel around. I'm in a strange bed. In the distance

I hear a dog bark, distant voices, *church bells* . . . and I realise I'm at the Infirmary. Relief wells up inside me and I want to laugh and cry at the same time.

A chair creaks and there's the *shush-shush* of curtains being opened. Pale sunshine pours through a window. I'm in a bedroom I don't recognise. There are pictures on the wall, a bookshelf, and a water jug and wash bowl on a table. A fire crackles in a pot-bellied stove.

Mrs Edington bends over me. 'Annie,' she says, placing a cool hand to my forehead. 'You're awake.'

'Yes . . .' I let out a huge yawn. 'How long have you been there?'

'All night, dear. I've not left your side. How are you feeling?'

'Better, thank you.'

'That eye still looks sore . . .'

'It's not too bad.'

'Good. I told James and the others of your return and they can hardly wait to see you.'

I settle back on the pillows. 'Where am I? I don't recognise this room.'

'You're in my house. This is the guest bedroom.'

'Oh. I don't remember coming here . . .'

'That's because you fell asleep in the bath.' Mrs Edington swipes some ointment from a tin and dabs it around my bruised eye. 'You've been dead to the world for nearly a day.'

'I'd like to get up now.'

'Are you sure? Do you feel strong enough?'

I nod. 'I want to see outside.'

Mrs Edington helps me out of bed and over to the window. She stands behind me, both hands resting on my shoulders as I stare at the stables, the Infirmary, and the rooftops and chimneys of Greenville.

'There, it's just the same as . . . as when you left all that time ago.'

'It does look the same,' I murmur. 'But it feels different.'

There's a long silence, then she says, 'I can't tell you how sorry I am. If I'd had even the slightest inkling of what those . . . *people* . . . were capable of I would never . . .' She kneels and turns me around. 'From now on you'll be living here with Mr Edington and me, and we're going to look after you as if you were our own daughter.'

'I'd like that.' My thoughts drift past Greenville, over woods and hills, all the way to the cabin. 'I'd like to see my family too.'

'Of course. As soon as you're strong enough I'll take you myself. They're all well, by the way. I've written your mother, telling her you're back with us now. I didn't mention anything about how you'd been . . . treated.'

'Good,' I say quietly. 'I don't want them to know about that.'

Mrs Edington guides me back to the bed and we sit side by side. 'What about me? Will you tell me what happened?'

What happened . . . Memories and emotions from the past two years crash over me. I hug myself as the shivers take hold. I'm cold, despite the fire; fearful, despite being safe.

'*Rurr, rurr, rurr . . . Rurr, rurr, rurr . . .*'

Mrs Edington holds me close but I don't stop shivering for a very long time.

30

I stop at the gate to gaze at the cabin, the barn and stable, the yard, the meadow and the woods beyond. At first glance everything looks just the same, but then I spy the sagging roofs, cracked boards and missing tiles. Time's left some scars on my old home, just as it has on me. When I think of the frightened girl I was when I left here two years ago, and all I've been through since . . . well . . . will my family even recognise me?

I've had two weeks to think about this first visit (they don't know I'm coming – it's going to be a complete surprise), enough time for my bruises to heal and to prepare myself for the changes I know I'll find. I've decided I don't want Ma to know about my ordeal with the Wolves. She's not to blame for what happened, but I know she'll feel guilty anyway. And what good would that do? No. It's my secret. My cross to carry.

The gate creaks. I walk slowly across the yard. The fields are brown, and I can tell only some have been prepared for sowing. It's a cold day, and the wind shreds the smoke as it emerges from the chimney and billows the sheets on the line.

The meadow's been cultivated for something or other. Potatoes maybe. There's no sign of Maple – the stable's empty and there's no dung on the ground. She must have died, poor thing.

It's so quiet . . . Where *is* everyone?

I give a cry as a man wearing filthy dungarees and the faint smell of manure emerges from the barn with a pitchfork over his shoulder – and for a lightning-flash moment I'm staring at Mr Wolf. My heart cranks up like a threshing machine and a panicked voice in my head screams run-*run-RUN*.

I've already taken a backward step before I realise this ain't Mr Wolf at all. I mean, of *course* it ain't! I'm still jittery, is all . . . As my heart slows, I see a slim middle-aged man with an unlit corncob pipe in his mouth and a surprised look on his be-whiskered face. 'Can I help you, Miss? You're way off track if you're looking for Woodland.'

Of course. This must be my stepfather.

'Oh, I ain't lost,' I say. 'S'matter of fact, I'm home.'

He puts down the pitchfork. 'Well now,' he says, peering closely at me, 'you must be Annie. Yes!' And his face creases into a smile. 'I can see the resemblance to Susan.' He wipes a hand on his dungarees and holds it out. 'I'm Joseph. And I am pleased to meet you.'

This – *he* – is going to take some getting used to, and I intend to form my opinion of him with clear eyes and dispassionate judgement. However, I see no reason to be rude, and I'm about to take his hand when the cabin door opens and Ma walks out.

She's looking over her shoulder and talking to someone in the kitchen. Like the cabin, at first glance she looks just the same, until I notice a thinness about her and more grey than brown in her hair. Seems these past two years have cost her ten.

'. . . don't be so foolish, Lydia. I was born in Pennsylvania, as you well know. I've never even *seen* a steamboat, let alone lived on one . . .' She turns round, sees me, and freezes.

There's a painful jolt in my heart when I see the web of care lines on her face. Somehow, I manage to speak over the lump in my throat. 'Howdy, Ma.'

'Phoebe,' she whispers. 'My dear child . . . Is it really you?'

'Course it is,' I say, feeling my face crease into a sort of crying-laughing-grimace. 'I'm here and, oh' – I swipe at the tears cascading down my face – 'I must look quite a sight.'

'Phoebe, my darling girl.' She's rigid, making no move towards me – perhaps she can't believe I'm really returned.

Sounds of consternation emerge from indoors.

'Who's out there?' That's Liz . . .

'Did Ma say, "Phoebe"?' John . . .

'Could it be . . . ?' Sarah Ellen . . .

'Well, don't just sit there, let's go and *see*!' Lydia!

Chairs scrape, plates rattle and my sisters and dear John

appear on the porch and spread out behind Ma; their expressions turn (at different rates, with Lydia being the quickest) from disbelief, to amazement, to happiness.

I can barely see through my tears. The sight of them all, looking older yet still somehow the same, robs me of my voice. Happiness fills me like melted butter as they surround then bundle me – a dizzy, laughing mess – into the cabin.

'Come on, Ma,' Lydia calls as she shoves me into a chair, 'who turned you into a statue?'

'It's all right,' John says, gently tugging her inside by the arm. 'She ain't a ghost. Go on – touch her. She's solid enough!'

They all sit down at the table and stare at me. Ma still looks like someone's hit her on the back of the head with a spade. She puts her hand on mine. 'You're right, John. She's not a ghost.'

My stepfather comes in, looking a bit awkward. 'I'll make some coffee.'

'You sit down, Father,' Sarah Ellen says. 'I'll make it.'

They call him Father . . .

'Well,' I say, looking around the cabin, 'this place looks just the same.'

'Cept it don't. It's clean and tidy, yes, but the windows are misty and cracked, the curtains frayed, and everyone's clothes look threadbare. Whatever did they spend Mr Wolf's money on if not on upkeeping this place?

'How'd you get here from Greenville?' Sarah Ellen asks.

'Mrs Edington dropped me off in the wagon. She's visiting some folks hereabouts,' I reply. 'But you know, Mr Edington's says that as soon as I'm used to riding his horse, I can come visit whenever I like.'

'Well, that sure would be fine,' Lydia beams, putting her arm over my shoulder and pulling me close.

'And how's Huldie?' I ask. 'D'you see her much?'

'Sure we do,' Lydia says. 'Whenever I'm in town on farm business I drop round, and the Fairheads visit every now and again.'

'She always asks after you, Annie,' Liz adds, and that news sure does warm my heart.

Ma's looking at me, worry in her eyes. 'You got my letter? About me remarrying?'

'I did.'

'Well, this is he. Mr Joseph Shaw. He's part of the family now.'

'And we didn't get to finish our introductions,' Mr Shaw says, standing up and extending his hand again. 'It sure is a pleasure to meet you, Annie.'

I stand too and shake his hand. 'Likewise.'

Ma sits by me and doesn't let go of my hand as my siblings run around and put lunch out. Bread, cheese, grits and coffee. I catch a glimpse of the larder and see it's as heartbreakingly bare as it ever was.

'So, d'you get my letters?'

'I did, every two weeks, and I read them to everyone,' Ma says. 'It did me good to hear how well you were doing. Are you going back to the Graces soon?'

'No, Ma,' I say. 'They . . . They don't need me any more. I'm living at the Infirmary now, back helping the Edingtons.' I bite my lip, dreading the answer to my next question. 'And the money they sent, was that useful?'

'Money?'

'The two dollars every two weeks,' I persist, feeling my voice vibrate with rising emotions, 'that came with each letter.'

'Oh no, Annie. We never got any money. Mr Grace wrote me before even your first letter arrived, saying he was sorry, but times were hard all of a sudden and they couldn't afford to send any.' Ma shakes her head sadly. 'Well, we know how that goes better than most, don't we? So I understood.'

I don't think there are words to describe what I feel. All that toil, all that misery I put up with on the condition that money was being sent here. I remember the times I watched him slip those dollar bills into the letters, and now I picture him taking them out again later. He probably laughed as he did it. Taking me for a fool for two miserable years and depriving my family of their due.

'Don't fret about it, dear,' Ma says, and it's strange, but as she looks at me it's like some of the creases disappear from her face. 'With God's help we got by, and by God's grace we're together again. And the best thing is, I see no reason why we need part in sadness again, and I can hardly express how happy that makes me.'

'You know, you ain't hardly changed a bit, Annie,' Liz says.

'I reckon she's gotten shorter,' Lydia grins. 'And I didn't believe that was possible.'

I give her my best frown. 'You'd best have kept my rifle polished like you promised.'

'Actually,' Sarah Ellen says, 'Father's been looking after it. Even took it to the woods a few times for a spot of hunting.'

'Didn't have much luck, though – never was much of a shot.' He casts me an unsure look. 'I hope you don't mind.'

'Naw, that's all right,' I say slowly. 'I'd rather it was being made use of.'

Ma takes the rifle down from over the fireplace and sets it against the table next to me. 'You should take this with you when you go. Get some fresh meat for those poor folks at the Infirmary.'

The moment I wrap my fingers around the cold metal barrel I realise just how *incomplete* I've felt without having it by my side.

Mr Shaw gets up, rummages in the chest and hands me Pa's old shot bag. 'There's fresh cartridges in there. Maybe you could take me up into the woods sometime, show me how it's done?'

'Sure,' I say. 'Sounds daisy.'

I look around at Ma, Lydia, Sarah Ellen, Liz, John – even 'Father', who everyone seems to hold in such affection – and imagine Pa and Mary Jane looking down on us. As the day passes, my anger and resentment about the money fades, the Wolves slink away to a lair deep in the darkest place in my mind (where I hope they'll stay, at least for a while), and I decide I'm going to live the rest of my life looking firmly forwards.

PART THREE

31

EARLY SUMMER 1873

I'm alone among the trees. The air is cool and full of forest smells: tree sap, thyme and oleander sage. My time slaving for the Wolves has made my body strong; I can hold Pa's rifle steady from the shoulder for ages before my aim drops.

My mind's changed too, but in ways harder to explain. Some days I feel hopeful for the future, and believe that because I survived the Wolves, I can survive anything. But when nightmares throw me into the snow with a pair of prowling, yellow-eyed wolves, I cannot always stifle the scream when I wake. I guess some scars run deeper than the ones on my skin.

I still work at the Infirmary (Mr Edington's put me in charge of the dairy herd and every morning I make sure every child has a tot of milk) but so long as I do my chores, I'm allowed to come and go, trap and hunt whenever I choose. It's a freedom I've never experienced, and I cherish it.

I was worried I might have lost the knack for hunting after so long without practice, but it came back pretty quick.

Why, just today I've filled my bag with half a dozen quail and a couple of grouse. I guess that's enough, so I shoulder my rifle, make my way out of the trees and onto the road to Greenville.

Hearing Ma's voice in my head, I smooth down my dress, wipe the mud from my boots and straighten my hat before I hit Main Street. I stop and peer at some pheasants hanging from a rack in the window of Katzenberger's General Store. Well now, *there's* an idea . . .

A bell tinkles as I open the door and stride up to the man behind the counter. A flicker of surprise passes over his moustachioed face when he sees my rifle. 'Afternoon, Miss,' he says, removing the toothpick from his mouth. 'Fine day, ain't it?'

'It sure is.'

'That's a fearsome looking iron you got there. That your pa's?'

'Sure ain't. Not any more. This is mine.'

'Huh,' he says, and there's that flicker of surprise again. 'So, you looking to sell it? I'll give you a fair price.'

'Sell my rifle?' I laugh. 'I can't imagine anything compelling me to do such a foolhardy thing.'

'Oh, well . . . So what *can* I do for you, Miss . . . ?'

'Miss Annie Mosey, and I have some business to discuss with Mr Katzenberger. He around?'

'Business, eh? Well, you're in luck, because I am Mr Charles

Katzenberger, owner and operator of this establishment. And, Miss Mosey, I am all ears.'

I jerk my thumb towards the window. 'Who supplies your game?'

'Local hunters, backwoods folk. Anyone who can aim and shoot and's in need of a dollar or two.'

'They all use shotguns, I bet.'

'Sure they do.'

'And riddle these fine birds with buckshot.'

Mr Katzenberger shrugs. 'I guess.'

'Leaving your paying customers to pick the lead out their mouths as they eat.'

'Folk expect that. These birds gotta be killed with *something*, and a shotgun'll get the job done as good as anything else.'

'Respectfully, Mr Katzenberger, I disagree. A rifle is superior when hunting game for the pot. All you need do after the kill is remove a single bullet, leaving nothing behind but prime, unspoiled meat.'

Mr Katzenberger leans both elbows on the counter. 'But none of them backwoods boys use a rifle.'

'But *I* do.' I grin and plonk my (slightly bloody) catch bag onto the counter. 'Go ahead – take a look.'

Frowning, Mr Katzenberger opens the bag and peers inside. 'Well, I'll be damned.' He pulls out a quail and examines the single bullet hole just below the neck. 'There must be half a dozen birds in here . . .'

'Now you see why I don't want to sell my rifle.'

He stares at me. 'This . . . This is *your* haul? *You* shot all these birds?'

I nod, relishing his surprise.

'You bagged 'em with that old muzzle-loader you got there?'

'Yes, sir.'

'And may I enquire just how'd you got to be so afly with a firearm?'

'My pa taught me, and he taught me well.'

Mr Katzenberger laughs and shakes his head. 'You'll have to forgive a coarse man his vernacular, Miss Mosey, but I'll be god-*damned*.' He spreads his hands wide. 'So, what's your proposal?'

'That I supply you with the finest game the forests of Darke County have to offer, and you pay me a fair price in return.' I tap my catch bag. '*Rifle*-shot, remember. So I'd politely ask for a lick more pay than you give those shotgun-totin' backwoods boys.'

Mr Katzenberger chuckles. 'You know, this morning I had no reason to think that this day would be any different to another. And then a girl no bigger than a corn nubbin comes in here with a gun taller'n she is, the biggest bag of birds I've ever seen, *and* a shrewd mind for business.' He points his toothpick at me. 'You know, you might just be the most surprising young woman who's ever walked into my store.'

'I'll take that as a compliment.'

'You should.' He holds out his hand. 'You got yourself a deal, Miss Mosey.'

Five minutes later I'm back on Main Street, holding onto the cash in my pocket and the joy in my heart. I've gotten myself an income!

32

The money I earn from hunting goes straight into a glass jar hidden under a floorboard in my room. I'm putting the lion's share aside for something *special*. It's going to take me ages to save enough – years, probably – but it'll be worth it in the end.

Today, however, I'm running errands in Greenville so I'm going to spend a dollar or two on DuPont gunpowder and some candy for my next visit to the cabin.

'Morning, Miss Mosey,' Mr Katzenberger says. 'No birds for me today?'

'Not today, Mr Katzenberger.' I hand him Mrs Edington's grocery list. 'Can you deliver all that by Friday?'

'Sure can,' he says, adding my list to a pile. 'You know, I'm glad you've paid me a visit.'

'Oh?'

'Fella came in yesterday and asked me to put this up in the window.' He unrolls a poster and lays it on the countertop. 'How's your reading?'

'Mrs Edington's been teaching me. I'm pretty good these days.'

'Well then. Take a look.'

I study the big black letters on the poster:

Annual Turkey Shoot

To commence in Strawberry, Ohio
On the farm of Mister Arthur Morgan
Saturday 17th August
All shootists welcome
Cash prizes

Mr Katzenberger taps the poster. 'Cash prizes, Miss Mosey. And I reckon, with your abilities, they're yours for the taking.'

'I ain't ever been to a turkey shoot. How'd they work?'

'It's simple enough. Contestants take turns shooting at a target and the one who hits closest to the bullseye wins.'

'That's it?'

'That's it.'

'Huh.' I think of my money jar. 'Where's Strawberry?'

'About fifteen miles away. I can take you in the wagon.'

I give a wry smile. 'That's mighty generous of you, Mr Katzenberger. Mighty generous *indeed*.'

'Well, not entirely generous.' He taps his nose and winks. 'I've no doubt some local muckety-muck'll be running a book on who'll win, and I ga-run-*tee* those country folk'll take one look at you and think you won't be able to shoot for spit.' He gives a hoot of laughter. 'They'll give me great odds, and I'll clean up!'

'Not if I lose,' I say with a frown.

The day of the turkey shoot's arrived and a highly jovial Mr Katzenberger is driving me along a bumpy path hedged with wheat fields towards Mr Morgan's farm. I had second (and third) thoughts this morning about going off with Mr Katzenberger; he's pretty much an unknown quantity to me, and look what happened the last time I was driven away by a man I didn't know.

But then the sensible part of my mind – the part that reassures me that the staring stranger across the street or the figure following me down the alleyway *ain't* Mr Wolf and there's nothing to be afraid of – reasserted itself and reminded me that I'm a more capable and independent person now (not to mention rifle-armed!) who can look after herself perfectly well, thank you very much. And so I took his politely proffered hand, climbed up next to him, and enjoyed the journey listening to him bloviate about this, that and the other.

Ahead, beneath a clear blue sky, is a cluster of red barns in a meadow all set up with gaily coloured tents and bunting. There's hay bales to sit on, pony rides for the children, a busy beer stall and several hogs roasting on spits.

Mr Katzenberger draws to a halt just inside the gate.

'Decent crowd,' he says, surveying the scene with approval. 'You'll have quite an audience.'

He's right. There must be a good few hundred folk milling about and enjoying the sunshine. 'They won't *all* be watching the shooting, will they?'

'Course they will!' he laughs. 'That's why they're here.'

A flurry of butterflies does circuits around my stomach. 'Maybe this time I should just watch,' I say, 'and come back when I've a better grasp of proceedings.'

Mr Katzenberger cups a hand behind his ear. 'Who's that talkin' about quitting? Cos it sure don't sound like the Miss Mosey I know.'

'But I ain't shot in front of *people* before,' I hiss. 'I reckon I need a lick more practice . . .' I don't meet his eye; I already feel a mite ashamed.

'Miss Mosey, you told me you started shooting at six years old. Was that a lie?'

'No, sir.'

'And how many birds and beasts you bagged since then?'

I shrug. 'Hundreds, I guess.'

'Right. You've had more than enough practice to knock any one of the boys competing here right onto their bee-hinds.'

'You just want me to shoot cos you think I'll win you some money.'

'True enough,' he chuckles, holding out my long rifle, 'but you stand to profit too.'

I think of the special thing I'm saving for. 'Of *course* I'm going to shoot,' I huff, taking the rifle. 'I was only horsing around.'

Mr Katzenberger grins. 'Thought as much. Now, you see that table yonder? You go on over there and register to compete while I stow the wagon and see about laying a bet.'

I follow his pointing finger to a chequered cloth-covered table with a portly, red-faced man sitting on one side, and a bunch of jawing, laughing men with shiny repeaters and breech-loading rifles on the other.

Mr Katzenberger must have seen the nervousness on my face. He crouches in front of me. 'You go on over there, Miss Mosey. You go on over and look him that's behind that table right in the eyeball, and you tell him your name. And don't you stop tellin' him until he writes it down along with all the rest.'

I nod, straighten my back, sling my rifle over my shoulder and march on over. It takes a bit of effort to push myself through the other shootists and I'm a bit out of breath when I reach the table.

'Good morning, sir,' I say with as much assurance as I can muster.

The red-faced man is poring over his ledger and doesn't even look at me, 'Morning, young lady. You lost?'

'Nope. I've come to register for the turkey shoot.'

'Excuse me?' he says, looking up at last.

'I said I'd like to register. For the turkey shoot.'

His face splits into a smile that I really don't care for. 'Are you playing a game with me, Missy?'

Missy? I don't care for *that*, either. 'No, sir. I've no time for games. I'm here to compete.'

I watch in cold surprise as what begins as a wheeze deep inside his chest slowly progresses into a sort of demented owl's hoot. It seems to go on forever and is most unseemly.

'Compete?' he gasps at long last. 'You? God have mercy on my soul! Now that is *funny*!'

If I had hackles, they'd be bristling. If I had no restraint, I'd punch him on the nose. I take a deep and calming breath, determined not to hand him the satisfaction of seeing me lose my temper.

'My name is Phoebe Anne Mosey,' I say. 'And I'd like you to put that down in your book there.'

Still snickering, the man shakes his head. 'No, no, no, Missy, that dog just won't hunt. Look around. You see any other little girls here? Because I sure don't. I only see grown men come to compete in a man's sport.' He waves a hand at me. 'I'm not entering you, so just run along and let me get about my business.'

I jab my finger onto one of the posters pinned to the table. 'Show me where it says on here that girls can't compete.'

He pauses, then says, 'It don't need to say it. Everyone takes it as read.'

'Well *I* don't!' I say, bristling good and proper now. '*All shootists welcome*, it says.' I unsling my rifle and slam it down on the table hard enough to make him jump. 'I'm a shootist, and I'm asking you to follow the directions on your own darn poster and put my name down.'

I realise my voice is raised enough to carry a fair way. A woman behind gives a nervous laugh. Conversations die away. Men turn towards me. I feel them assessing me, judging me, wondering who I am and why I'm making a fuss.

I keep my eyes locked on my counterpart and say, 'Phoebe Anne Mosey. That's my name.' The silence drags on, but I'm not moving. No *sir*.

'I think you'd better do as she asks, Will,' a man to my left says, 'or she might just shoot you right out of your chair.'

A few people laugh at that. I don't drop my gaze. 'Phoebe. Anne. Mosey.'

'Go on. Put her name down,' a man with a repeater under his arm says. 'I want to see how she fares.'

'And she *is* right,' a woman adds. 'It says shootist on the poster, and she's got a rifle. That qualifies her s'far as I'm concerned.' There's a general murmur of agreement.

The man – Will – is even redder now and huffing like a steam train. 'But we've never allowed a girl to compete before.'

'I bet none's ever come forward to ask,' the woman retorts.

'It's not right, not proper—'

'I don't care one bit about what you think's proper,' I say, surprised but pleased that the crowd's siding with me. 'There ain't no reason in the world why I shouldn't be allowed to shoot just because God saw fit to make me female.'

Will peers around at all the people backing my play and, seeing himself as a one-man minority, scribbles my name in the book. 'We'll see how much of a shootist you are when you get out on the range,' he mutters.

I guess I should feel victorious, but actually I'm exhausted. And *angry*. Why should I have to fight just to get what a man takes for granted? Will it be the same every time I want to enter a contest? The unfairness makes me want to scream. Needing a quiet spot to gather my thoughts before the contest (which I'm now utterly determined to win), I shoulder my rifle and march through the still-interested crowd.

As I pass, the man with the repeater touches me on the arm. 'Pardon me, Miss. Is that the rifle you'll be using?'

'Sure is.'

'Mind if I take a look?'

I hesitate before passing it over. He examines it with a practised and respectful eye before giving it back.

'It's a fine old iron,' he nods. 'But it won't match the modern firearms we're all using. The targets here are ranged at one hundred yards. What's that rifle accurate up to? Fifty yards? Seventy at best, I reckon.'

'That depends,' I say.

'Oh yeah? On what?'

'Why, on who's shooting, of course.'

He grins and tips his hat. 'I'll see you on the range.'

I find Mr Katzenberger near a vittles stall. 'Get yourself registered?' he asks, handing me a beef sandwich and a bottle of lemonade.

'Just about. Honestly, you'd think they'd never seen a girl with a gun before.'

'They probably haven't,' he chuckles. 'That's an interesting precedent you've set today.'

I don't know what that means and I'm too preoccupied to ask.

'We've got half an hour,' he continues. 'That's time enough for lunch, and a quick recce of the battlefield. Come on.'

33

Turns out there's enough contestants to make six sets of four shooters. Will's in charge of who goes on what set, and in what order the sets'll shoot. He's put my set up first – probably because he thinks I'm going to lose and just can't wait to see it.

Well, we'll just see about *that*.

My rivals and I have taken position on the shooting field, while Will marches to the far end and nails a paper target to a wooden frame. I take a little bit of notice of the men I'm shooting against (which includes the friendly repeater-owner whose name, it turns out, is Mr Reid), but mostly I'm concentrating my mind and trying to shut out distractions.

Which ain't easy.

Seems everyone attending the fair's gathered to watch, maybe because they want to see how the strange girl with the antique muzzle-loader does. My rivals are checking their weapons, rolling their shoulders, or turning to wave to friends in the crowd. They look relaxed, and I guess they've competed in turkey shoots before.

I try to ignore the sick sensation bubbling up in my stomach.

If I miss a shot in the woods there's no one around to see. Here? There's a whole bunch of people watching, including Will, and I *really* don't want to mess up in front of him.

He's nearly finished fiddling with the target, so I set about loading my rifle. Pouring the powder, ramming home the ball, priming the pan . . . It's a routine I've done countless times and I find it actually soothes my nerves some. In fact, by the time Will's returned to address the crowd, my rifle's primed and I'm feeling pretty good.

I glance at the gathered crowd and see Mr Katzenberger right at the front. He gives me a wink; I send back a smile.

'Ladies and gentlemen,' Will says, puffing up like he's the biggest toad in the puddle, 'it's time for the Turkey Shoot!' There are a few cheers and claps from the crowd. 'Each man' – he gives me a filthy look – 'or *otherwise*, steps up to this here line and has three shots at the target. I will number each bullet hole between contestants to keep track of whose is whose. Closest shot to the bullseye wins.' He gestures to us. 'First set, take your shots!'

Mr Reid raises his eyebrows at me. 'Would you like to go first, Miss?'

'That's kind, but you all go ahead.'

I watch carefully as Mr Reid steps up to the mark, takes aim, fires three shots from his repeater then re-joins our group. Will approaches the target with a ruler, makes his marks on the paper and steps away.

'Mr Reid didn't quite make his Jack,' he calls, 'Closest shot is one inch from the bullseye.' The crowd claps. Mr Reid grins and tips his hat. The second rival steps up, takes his shots and retreats looking a bit downcast. Will checks and calls back, 'Mr Reid is still closest. Next shooter!' The third takes his turn, and Will informs us that Mr Reid remains the one to beat.

'Final shooter,' Will calls. As I step up to the mark, he pretends to duck and scurries off to one side. 'Reckon I'll stand further away for this one. Don't want to get hit!'

I swallow my annoyance, knowing the best way to show him up is to make him announce my victory. I spread my legs to get a solid base, raise the rifle, cock the hammer and sight down the barrel. My back's ramrod straight, my arms rock steady, the stock warm against my cheek. Will, my rivals, the crowd, even the prospect of failure all drift away. It's just me, my rifle, and the target.

At this distance the target's about the size of a picture postcard, but my keen eyes see the black circles clear as daylight. I imagine my bullet speeding from the muzzle in a plume of smoke and piercing that bullseye right through the centre.

I line up the barrel, let out a breath, and squeeze the trigger.

We're on our way back to Greenville and Mr Katzenberger's yet to stop laughing.

'Well, didn't that just cap the climax!' he says, rocking back and forth in his seat. 'A bullseye on your first shot! No need to even reload! I *told* you you'd knock 'em on their bee-hinds!'

'I might have got a bit lucky.'

'Luck, my battered hat! You were a country mile better than those boys even with your pa's old rifle.'

I shrug but can't help giving Mr Katzenberger a big smile. 'It did feel good to take the prize money.'

'That ruddy-lookin' fella looked positively sick about it!' he says before succumbing to another bout of mirth. 'I had so much fun today, the money I won feels like a bonus.' He hands me a ten-dollar bill, which I gratefully accept. 'So, you want to do this again? There's another shoot in New Harrison next month.'

'Sure,' I say, rather relishing the prospect. 'Why not?'

34

WINTER 1873

I've been to turkey shoots all over Darke County and I swear there's a 'Will' kicking up a fuss at every one. Luckily, most of 'em are so weak north of the ears that they couldn't hit the ground with their hat in three throws, and they never stop me competing no matter how hard they try. And let me confide – it tastes sweet as apple pie every time they have to pony up the prize money. I don't even get anxious before shooting any more; I've won pretty much every contest so far and my jar's filling up fast.

Course, getting to be the boss takes a lot of practice, and I'm back and forth to Mr Katzenbergers' all the time for more gunpowder and shot.

Today I'm gazing longingly at the guns all racked up behind the counter while he deals with some customers. Remingtons, Winchesters and Marlins, Lancasters, Parkers and Spencers – some decorated with fancy engravings and carved stocks, others quite plain and practical-looking. There's pistols gleaming under the glass countertop too: Smith & Wesson six-shooters, Colts and Renettes. I've never shot a pistol before and I doubt they're much use for hunting, but I'd love to give it a try . . .

'See anything you like?'

I was so lost in thought I hadn't noticed Mr Katzenberger stroll up behind me. 'Pretty much everything you've got back there,' I reply.

He lifts up the counter flap and runs a practised eye along the gun rack. 'Let's see . . . Ah, this one might suit.' He picks up a short-barrelled rifle and sets it down on the countertop. 'The Winchester Model 1866 lever-action repeating rifle. Lightweight, reliable and accurate – perfect for a game-hunter like you.'

I put it to my shoulder. It's only about half the length and weight of my long rifle, but still feels solid and well-balanced.

'It takes forty-four calibre rimfires,' he continues. 'You slide them into the loading gate in the side there – see? And after loosing off a shot you just push that lever behind the trigger guard forward and it chambers another round for you. No more powder-pouring with this beauty. Go on, have a go. It ain't loaded.'

I aim at the floor (just in case) and pull the trigger. There's a *snick* as the firing pin hits the empty chamber, then I use the front of my bottom three fingers to push the lever forward until it stops, then let it snap back into place. I do it again, faster this time. *Snick, push, snap; snick, push, snap; snick, push, snap.* I feel the firing mechanism click and slide every time I repeat the action.

'It's called a Yellow Boy because of that bright brass receiver,' Mr Katzenberger says. 'So, what do you reckon?'

I put it back on the countertop and trail my fingers over the smooth wooden stock. 'How much?'

'Thirty-five dollars.'

I shake my head. 'I'm saving up for something else right now. I can't afford this as well.'

Mr Katzenberger draws a hand down over his drooping moustaches. 'Mm, well, I've been thinking, Miss Mosey. Imagine how much game you'd be able to bring in with a repeater like this. More than with your old muzzle-loader, for sure.'

'Oh, for sure.'

'So, how 'bout this? You take that there Winchester away with you today, along with some Henry rimfires' – he produces a box of bullets from under the counter – 'and set about your business in the woods. And every time you bring me a haul, I'll deduct from your fee, say, twenty-five cents in the dollar. And we carry on like that until you've paid back the thirty-five bucks.'

I stare at him. 'You mean I can take it . . . today?'

'Sure. I trust you. And you'll be able to bring in more birds for me to sell, so we'll both benefit. Think of it as a pragmatic and sensible progression of our business relationship. What d'you say?'

I grin and pick up the repeater. 'I think you're going to need a bigger window rack.'

35

FALL 1874

At long last, after a bunch more turkey shoot victories and countless hunting trips bagging game to sell, I've finally scraped together the money I need for my *special purpose*. Yesterday I took my money jar to the bank in Greenville and proudly asked the teller to change it for twenty-four ten-dollar bills. That's two-hundred and forty dollars – a fortune! – and every cent earned with my rifle.

It's a glorious afternoon for a ride on Maggie, Mr Edington's lively brown-and-white American Paint. I've got a basket of food tied to the saddle, Pa's rifle over my shoulder and a new hat with a silver star on the brim. Right now, and especially today, I am happy. I stop whistling and smile as I canter into the yard and see Ma pegging out some sheets.

'Well now, this is a nice surprise,' she says, taking Maggie's reins and tying her to the porch.

'Just thought I'd drop by and see how you all are,' I reply, slipping down and giving Ma a kiss.

'You're up to something,' she frowns. 'I can tell.'

'Me? Never!' I hold up the basket. 'I've brought lunch.'

'You shouldn't have,' Ma tuts.

'But I *wanted* to.'

'And I know better than to try and stop you.' She smiles. 'Look at you with Pa's old rifle. He sure would've loved to see you make such good use if it.'

'It does me proud. Mr Katzenberger sells the game I provide all over the place these days, even as far as Cincinnati.'

'Well, fancy that. Come along in then.'

The cabin's spotless as always, but the worn curtains and cracked windows still ain't been fixed.

'Look who's come to see us,' Ma says.

Father gets up from the table and beams. 'Why, hey there, Annie' – only Ma calls me Phoebe these days – 'you've swell timing. We were just about to eat.'

'Afternoon, Father,' I say. 'And my timing ain't accidental. I'm starving.'

'Now, what have you got in that basket?' he asks.

'Nice things.' I whip off the cloth to reveal fresh bread, butter, cheese, thick slices of ham wrapped in paper, bottles of beer and soda, and an apple pie.

Ma kisses the top of my head and lays out plates, cups and cutlery.

'I received a letter from Lydia the other day,' she says. 'Our newlywed has invited us to visit in Cincinnati next month. Do you think the Edingtons will be able to spare you?'

'I hope so. I'm dying to see her and find out how Mr Stein has tamed her.'

'Oh, I don't think she's anywhere near *tamed*,' Ma says. 'Anyway, I can't spare the time to go, much as I'd like to.'

'Well, I think you *should* go,' Father says. 'I can pick up the slack while you're away.'

'There's too much to do!' Ma exclaims. 'Until we can afford some extra hands we need to pull together, as always.'

'Where are John and the girls?' I ask as we help ourselves to the food.

'Sarah Ellen and Liz are visiting Mrs Francis to make sure she's looking after herself since she was sick,' Ma says, handing Father a bottle of beer. 'They'll be sorry they missed you.'

'And John's working in the top field, struggling with that darn plough,' Father says. 'I'll set some of this aside for them all.'

'Oh good. I'll go see him before I go. How's the farm?'

Ma and Father exchange glances. 'We're all right,' Father says stoutly. 'Don't you worry about us.'

'That's what I keep telling your sisters,' Ma says. 'That they're not to stay here because of us. I won't clip their wings.'

'I guess it's the mortgage on this place that's the problem,' I say.

Ma closes her eyes; Father places a hand over hers. 'It's a noose around our neck,' she says. 'Always has been.'

'We're making the payments, but it don't leave much for anything else,' Father adds.

'Well,' I say, unable to wait any longer, 'how about this?'

I take the money roll from my pocket and place it between them on the table.

They stare at it. Father's mouth actually drops open.

'What's that?' they both say.

'That's two hundred and forty dollars. It's yours. My gift to you, to pay off what you owe on this place, and maybe have a party if there's anything left over.'

Ma touches the money and seems surprised to find it solid. 'But how . . . ?'

'I robbed the bank in Greenville,' I say. 'Posse'll be here any minute, so you'd best get spending.'

'Oh, hush now,' Ma says. 'Is this all from your shooting?'

'Every cent.'

'How long did it take you to earn?'

'That don't matter. It's yours now. So, will you take it?'

'I will.' Ma picks up the money. 'Oh Joseph, just think what this means. No more scraping every month to make payments.'

'We could buy a cow or fix the roof,' Father adds, drawing Ma to her feet.

'You could do both,' I say, clapping my hands as Father takes Ma on an actual turn around the room, 'and more besides.'

'I can't wait to tell the children,' Ma says, returning to the table a bit out of breath. 'Oh, after so many years of hard-scrabble' – she shakes her head – 'I can hardly imagine the change this will bring to our lives.'

'The first thing I prescribe for you, Susan,' Father says, 'is resting easy and enjoying life more. And what better way than you girls going to visit Lydia?'

'Perhaps,' Ma says, looking unsure.

'Not perhaps,' I say. 'We're going. We can stop off to see Huldie on the way then take the train. It'll be an adventure!'

Ma smiles. 'My clever Phoebe. You know, I have another idea for what we can use some of this money for.'

'What's that?'

'You remember the day you left – what, four years ago? – I said we'd get a photograph taken when we were together again?'

'Sure, I remember.'

'Well, why don't we do that? To celebrate the happier times we Moseys have to look forward to?'

I kiss her on the cheek. 'I think that's a grand idea.'

36

LATE FALL 1876

'There's a letter come for you, Annie,' Lydia says, passing me an envelope over the remains of our breakfast.

Ma (under Father's orders), Liz, Sarah Ellen and I are once again visiting Lydia and her husband Joe in Oakley, Cincinnati. We come fairly often these days now that Ma and Father can afford help on the farm, and we always drop in on dear Huldie – who's growing up to be a fine, well-educated girl with the Fairheads – on the way to Greenville train station.

Joe's an ambitious man from Germany who's quite the muckety-muck in the Cincinnati building trade. I sometimes ask him (only half-jokingly) how he puts up with Lydia's frivolous ways, but he just laughs and says they're the opposite sides of the same coin, different in many ways yet still complementary parts of a whole.

'Well,' Liz says, 'open it then!'

Frowning, I check the envelope and see my name is indeed on the top line of the address. 'Whoever could it be from? I mean, who knows I'm here?'

'Probably a secret admirer,' Lydia says, spreading a dollop

of strawberry preserve on her bread. 'A romantic poet who's too shy to talk to the fierce markswoman he's admired from afar, and who's decided to profess his deathless passion for you in a love letter.'

'Oh, really,' Ma tuts. 'I cannot fathom where you got your absurd imagination from, young lady.'

'If a man lacks the sand to speak his feelings to my face then he ain't no kind of man,' I say. 'Anyway, I don't have any secret admirers.'

'He wouldn't be a secret admirer if you knew about him, would he?' Lydia says.

'Besides,' Sarah Ellen laughs, 'a crack shot you may be, Annie, but when it comes to love you sure are short-sighted for a sixteen-year-old. Why, you'd be the last to realise if a man was trying to court you.'

'I'm too busy to be worrying about that sort of fiddle faddle,' I grumble.

'Urgh,' Lydia groans. 'You're hopeless!'

Even Ma raises an interested eyebrow when I open the envelope and read the letter. 'It's from a Mr Frost,' I say. 'Says he owns the Bevis House Hotel in Cincinnati and is a friend of Mr Katzenberger. He's asking if I would pay him a visit because he has a business proposal for me.' I turn the letter over between my fingers. 'I wonder what it could be?'

'Not as interesting as a secret admirer,' Lydia says, sounding deeply disappointed.

'Why don't we go this afternoon?' Liz says. 'I'm dying to explore the city some more.'

'All right,' I reply. 'And there's bound to be a gunsmith we can visit as well.'

Lydia frowns and with a remarkable approximation of Ma's voice says, 'I simply don't know where you get your absurd obsession with firearms from, young lady.'

Next morning after Joe leaves for work, Ma and us girls head into the bustling sprawl of Cincinnati. Some of the buildings are so tall I have to crane my neck to see their rooftops. The wide streets are lined with stores, restaurants, saloons and theatres, and teem with people who all seem to be in the most terrible hurry. Of course, Lydia's perfectly at home here – a real city lady. As for me, much as I enjoy the stimulation, I prefer the country.

After a turn along the Ohio River to watch the big white steamboats churn through the water like floating wedding cakes, Lydia herds us onto a horse-drawn streetcar. Into the heart of the city we go, rattling merrily along, until we reach a rather grand building with a portico and a sign up in lights that reads 'Bevis House Hotel'.

'Here we are,' Lydia says. 'This is Mr Frost's place. We can take tea here while Annie unravels the mystery of the letter.'

'All right,' I reply. 'I'll come find you when I'm done.'

As the others head into the hotel tea room, I tell the smartly-dressed woman at the front desk my name, and that I'm here to see Mr Frost, at his request.

'Just one moment, Miss Mosey,' she says before disappearing through a door. She reappears a moment later and beckons me into a large office with wood-panelled walls and windows overlooking the street. A middle-aged man, whose striped (and rather garish) suit strains over an impressive stomach, gets up and extends a hand over his desk.

'Miss Mosey,' he booms. 'It is a pleasure to meet you. Thank you for taking the time to pay me a visit.'

'Not at all, Mr Frost,' I say, shaking his hand. 'Your letter intrigued me.'

'Good, good.' He smiles and indicates to a chair.

Mr Frost seems jovial enough at first glance, and him being friends with Mr Katzenberger (who I've grown to trust implicitly) counts in his favour. However, as with all people, I'm reserving judgement until I've a sense of his character, and his intentions. I know most people ain't bad like the Wolves, but my experience at their hands (and fists) has taught me the benefits of caution.

'Thank you.' I sit on the edge of the chair, look Mr Frost in the eye, and wait.

The door opens and the woman from the front desk enters carrying a tray with cups, a coffee pot and a sugar bowl. I look around the office as she pours and notice a stag's head mounted above the door.

'D'you hunt, Mr Frost?'

'Animals? Hell, no. I'm a city dude, with soft hands.' He smiles and shows me his palms. 'But I do hunt. Oh, yes indeed.'

The smile's still playing around his lips, and I guess he wants me to ask. I withhold a sigh and oblige. 'What do you hunt, sir?'

'Ha! Profits, Miss Mosey. Profits!' He waits for the woman to leave before continuing. 'Now, our mutual friend Charlie Katzenberger told me you'd be up visiting your sister, and that fact got my mind a-cooking. You see, I've been buying your game from Charlie for years, and my hotel guests love it. Rifle shot, no pellets to break their teeth on – just fine, succulent meat.'

'I'm glad you're satisfied,' I say, wishing he'd reach his point.

'He also said you've won every turkey shoot you've entered. That true?'

'Pretty much. Got to the point now that most won't let me compete.' I give a wry smile. 'When I first started, organisers didn't want me shooting because I'm a woman. Nowadays they don't want me shooting because I'm too good for the men I go up against.'

Mr Frost lights a cigar, puffs a few times and regards me

through the smoke. 'You know,' he says, 'you are not at *all* what I expected.'

Seems like he's not fixing to oblige my desire for brevity, so I raise my eyebrow, just like Ma does when she's quizzical. 'Oh? What *were* you expecting?'

'Oh, hell,' he laughs, 'I hardly like to say now that I've clapped eyes on you!'

'Go ahead, Mr Frost. I don't shock easy.'

'Well, if you must know, I pictured some wild creature from the backwoods, decked out in hides and fur and spitting tobacco all over the place.'

'Is that what Mr Katzenberger told you?'

'Heck, no! He didn't tell me much, 'cept about your uncanny skill with a rifle. I guess I just ain't got a frame of reference to picture what a *fe*-male sharpshooter looks like.'

'And that's what you pictured?'

He holds up his hands. 'Respectfully, I did. But here you sit, perfectly presentable and civilised.'

'Am I then a disappointment to you, Mr Frost?'

'Not at all. Not at *all*. You're a surprise, is all, and that is to your credit.'

The coffee's strong enough to float a pony, the cigar smoke's making my eyes itch, and Mr Frost's prevarications are wearing on my nerves.

'Sir, I have other business to attend to this afternoon' – I don't – 'and I still have no notion as to why you've asked me here.'

Mr Frost stubs out his cigar. 'Quite right, quite right. Let's get to it, shall we? First of all, rest assured, my impending offer will benefit us both.'

'I'm listening, Mr Frost,' I say, while thinking, *I should darn well hope it does.*

'There's a big fair this weekend, right here in Cincinnati.'

'Sure, I've seen the posters.'

'Now, there's a trick shot specialist in town, goes by the name of Frank Butler. He's offering a fifty-dollar prize to anyone at the fair who can beat him at clay pigeon shooting.'

I give a low whistle. 'Fifty dollars? That's a lot to lay on the line.'

'Ah, well, that's the thing. Butler's good. *Professional.* Every challenger pays him five dollars, and I'd estimate he beats ninety-nine out of a hundred of 'em.' Mr Frost wags a finger at me. 'But, from what Charlie tells me, I'm willing to bet you might be the one out of the hundred who wins.'

Fifty dollars . . . I could pay off what I owe Mr Katzenberger for Yellow Boy and also be halfway to buying myself that Colt Peacemaker I've been daydreaming about.

'Well? What do you reckon, Miss Mosey?'

'I reckon I'd be a fool to let such an opportunity slip by.'

Mr Frost grins and claps his hands – I've never seen a

happier man. 'If ever a fella says Miss Annie Mosey's one to shirk a challenge, I'll gladly spit in his eye.'

'Fifty dollars is fifty dollars,' I say mildly. 'And I'm guessing you'll be placing a wager on me? At generous odds too, considering I'm an unknown here in Cincinnati?'

'Well now,' Mr Frost says with a knowing smile, *'there's* a notion . . .'

37

'That's Frank Butler over there,' Mr Frost says.

Along with a growing crowd of eager spectators, Ma, Liz, Sarah Ellen, Mr Frost and I are standing by a low rope fence separating us and all the fun of the Cincinnati Fair from a grass field where the shooting contest is to take place. I follow Mr Frost's finger to a dapper young gentleman wearing a dark suit, standing in the field by a table all laid out with shotguns and shotshell boxes. He's ignoring the crowd and using a shammy to polish a Parker Brothers side-by-side double-barrelled shotgun. Nice piece. The gun, I mean.

'What does he look like?' Ma asks. 'I can't see that far.'

'He's quite the tall drink of water,' Lydia replies approvingly. 'But don't let that put you off, Annie dear.'

'Huh. As if I'd let *that* happen.'

And it won't. I can appreciate a man who's easy on the eye (and at first glance Mr Butler *is* a handsome fellow) but I'm here with one purpose only: to win his fifty dollars.

It's a beautiful day, and it seems most of Cincinnati's turned out to enjoy the fair. We've dressed up for the occasion; Liz spent most of yesterday evening letting out the sleeves of my best dress so I can move free and easy when shooting.

Mr Frost's carrying Yellow Boy and my shot bag for me because I don't want to tip my hand that I'm competing until the last moment.

'What's going on over there, Mr Frost?' Sarah Ellen asks, pointing to four men tending to some metal contraptions further away in the field.

'They're the launchers, Miss,' he replies. 'They're spring-loaded, and when the shooter cries "pull" the operators'll send a disc of clay a-flying through the air. And that's what Butler and your sister will be aiming at. Most hits out of twenty-five wins.'

'But you've never tried clay pigeons before, have you, Phoebe?' Ma frowns.

'Nope, but I've shot birds on the wing.' I pause, then add, 'I reckon I'll watch a few rounds before presenting myself though.'

Mr Frost nods. 'I'd say that's a sound idea.'

The crowd's getting thick, there must be hundreds lined up to watch. Mr Butler's still polishing his guns, cool as a cucumber. I'm excited and nervous; this is a big crowd to lose in front of.

'See over there?' Mr Frost points to a group of a dozen men on the other side of the rope, toting, loading and checking their shotguns. 'There's them ninety-nine out of a hundred I told you about.'

Since picking us up in his shiny black barouche this morning, Mr Frost has been nothing but kind and courteous: buying us all sodas and escorting us through the fair with humour and charm. He might be a bit of a blow-hard, but I've quite warmed to him.

Frank Butler turns and strides towards his audience. Everyone goes quiet.

Mr Frost slips a five-dollar bill into my hand. 'Butler's fee, with my compliments. Now I'm off to find who's running the book and place my wager on you. Good luck!'

'Before you go, Mr Frost . . .' Ma hesitates, then says, 'I've never done such a thing before' – she dips her hand in her bag and pulls out three dollar bills – 'but would you place this on my Phoebe?'

'It'll be my pleasure.' Mr Frost takes the money, tips his hat, and disappears into the crowd.

We all stare at Ma, who's looking quite flushed.

'Who are *you* all of a sudden?' Lydia asks.

'Well,' Ma says, reddening even more, 'if I am going to gamble, it'll be on my girls.'

We all press close to take her hands and kiss her cheeks, and by the time she shoos us away, Frank Butler's standing close to the rope.

He throws three glass balls, each about the size of a crab

apple, high into the air. He waits a beat then slick as grease draws a Smith & Wesson Model 3 six-shooter from his belt and fires thrice. The balls explode in clouds of powder – one red, one white, one blue. The crowd gasps. So do I.

'Ladies and gentlemen,' he says, tucking his smoke wagon back into his belt, 'welcome to the show. My name is Mr Frank Butler. The national press have called me a champion sharp-shooter and the most illustrious of dead-shots.' He spreads his arms. 'And who am I to argue?' There's laughter, and I have to admit that he's quite the showman. 'But I'm not asking you to believe what's said in the papers. I'm here to prove myself to you, the fine people of Cincinnati, with action. Five bucks earns you the chance to show your skills, and there's a fifty-dollar prize to any man who outshoots me.'

'Or woman,' Lydia mutters, giving my hand a squeeze.

'So,' Mr Butler says, 'who's my first challenger?'

Accompanied by a cheer from his friends, a burly man with a shotgun strides up and hands Mr Butler the money.

'Ladies and gentlemen,' Mr Butler says, 'give this brave competitor a round of applause!'

The burly man exchanges a few words with Mr Butler and they stroll away from the fence to stand next to each other. The launchers, operators and stacks of clay pigeons are some way in front and to their left.

Mr Butler shouts, 'Pull!'

I watch carefully as the operator trips a lever. The launcher snaps, sending a clay disc a-sailing in a high, fast arc. Mr Butler raises his shotgun, fires when the disc is at its fullest height and blows it into a thousand pieces. The crowd cheers.

I calculate just how fast I'll need to react; those clay pigeons move quick and follow a different sort of path to a bird launching straight up from the ground. This is going to be tricky . . .

The challenger raises his shotgun, shouts 'Pull!'. He hits the pigeon, but only on his second shot. The crowd cheers again.

In the end, Frank Butler wins by hitting all twenty-five pigeons, and the challenger trudges back to the not-so-sympathetic comfort of his friends. And so it goes: challenger after challenger (all men, of course) stride out full of beans, get beat, then tramp back again five dollars poorer.

I'm most interested in the contestants who shoot well. I want to know what they do wrong so I can avoid the same mistakes. Seems to me they start off strong, matching Mr Butler. Then, when they're deep into the match, *that's* when they lose their nerve and miss a shot – and it's downhill from there.

I also see how calm Mr Butler is. Course, he's used to all this – the crowds, the competition, taking dozens of shots one after the other. It's a big advantage he has over ordinary folk, and I realise if I'm to redress the balance I need to get under his skin.

After a dozen victories, Mr Butler asks again if anyone wants to accept his challenge, and this time no one answers. 'All right then,' he declares. 'Then I thank you for your hospitality,' and he turns to pack up his gear. This is it. I just need to put my jangling nerves aside and trust in the skill Pa saw in me all those years ago.

'What's wrong, Annie?' Liz asks. 'You changed your mind?'

'Course not. I'm just waiting for the right moment . . . which I think . . . is about . . . *now*.' I whisper a quick prayer, shoulder my rifle, step lightly over the rope and trip right on up to Mr Butler.

'I accept your challenge,' I say, loud enough for the crowd to hear.

Mr Butler turns round . . . and stares.

38

Well, seems I've succeeded in catching the weasel asleep.

'Can you hear me, sir?' I say, enjoying his surprised look. 'I said I'd like to accept your challenge.'

When he still doesn't speak, I slip my five dollars into his suit's top pocket. The crowd laughs at this, and I can honestly say that I'm beginning to enjoy myself.

'But, you're . . . I mean . . . I've never competed against a girl . . .'

'And I've never shot clay pigeons before, so this is a day of firsts for the both of us.'

'Listen, Miss . . . ?'

'Mosey. Annie Mosey.'

'Miss Mosey. Are you sure you want to do this? Five dollars is a lot of money, and I feel bad taking it from you . . .'

'Huh . . . S'funny, because when it comes time for me to take your fifty, I won't feel bad at *all*.'

'But, Miss, you ain't even using the right kind of firearm. That there's a rifle.'

Giving him my sweetest smile, I say, 'I think you'll find it suits my needs.'

The launcher operators are gawking at me, just as nonplussed as Mr Butler. I unshoulder Yellow Boy.

Now, I know many folk who watch me shoot for the first time reckon I'll lose just because I'm a girl, and I take pride and pleasure in proving such foolish expectations wrong. But this is a city crowd – there's *hundreds* watching. What's more, Mr Butler's challenge caused enough of a stir to be mentioned in the newspapers (Mr Frost showed me the articles), and chances are there are reporters here to see what's shaking.

If I fail today, a great many people will know about it.

I take a breath and remind myself that I'm not trying to shoot a turkey to feed my starving family like when I was a little girl. This is just a contest. Heck – I didn't even have to put up my own five dollars.

Forget the crowd. Forget failure.

Just think about the shot.

I rack a round into the chamber and shout 'Pull!'

There's a snap as the launcher sets my target flying. I lift my rifle, tracking a little ahead of the pigeon until it flattens out at the top of its arc. I squeeze the trigger, and through the smoke plume see it shatter into shards and dust.

There's a delicious pause before the crowd cheers. Feeling some relief that I didn't foul up, I turn and drop a curtsey.

Mr Butler's staring at me like I'm some creature from a fairy story. 'Your shot,' I say, racking another rimfire. 'Good luck.'

He grits his teeth. 'Pull!' he calls, and a half-breath later his pigeon explodes. The crowd *oohs* and claps. I shout 'Pull!' before his shards have even landed and destroy the pigeon.

More claps and cheers, louder this time. There's a line of sweat glistening beneath the brim of Mr Butler's hat.

'Pull!' *Bang!* He hits.

'Pull!' *Bang!* I hit.

I allow myself a glance over my shoulder and see Ma with her hands clasped under her chin and my sisters clapping along with everyone else. Oh *boy*, what a day this is turning out to be!

Frank shouts 'Pull!' and another pigeon goes down in bits.

'Pull!' I echo, and my pigeon follows suit.

And so it goes, one pigeon after the other destroyed to the sound of the cheering crowd, until we're down to the last round. I sense Mr Butler's disquiet. I've matched him, shot for shot. What's more, I'm hitting my pigeons a second or two earlier in their flight than he is, proving I'm faster.

'What happens if we both hit our next targets?' I ask.

'We keep going until one of us misses,' Mr Butler replies, dabbing his brow with a handkerchief.

'Fair enough. Pull!'

The pigeon launches with a clatter. I watch it arc through

the air, a spinning grey disc against the bright blue sky, and snap off a shot. The crowd roars as it shatters into powder.

Mr Butler loads his shotgun, forehead creased with concentration. 'Pull!' The pigeon flies, he fires . . . and the pigeon continues, unharmed, to land with a thump in the grass. He shakes his head as if trying to clear it, then picks up a roll of bills and hands it to me without a word.

'Thank you. A close contest,' I say, and exit the field of battle on shaking legs.

39

It takes a while to work my way through the crowd on account of all the people wanting to congratulate me – although I think some were in such a state of disbelief that it was a female who beat Mr Butler they wanted a closer look to ensure I wasn't just a man in a dress.

I head on over to Mr Frost, who's standing near a test-your-strength machine counting a wad of money.

'What a show, what a *show*!' he beams, handing Ma her winnings (which she immediately splits between Liz, Lydia and Sarah Ellen) and me a ten-dollar bill. 'A well-deserved extra for you, Miss Mosey, for fulfilling every bit of your promise.'

'Why, thank you, Mr Frost. That's most kind.'

Sixty dollars for a half hour's work? My *word*!

'I predict a bright future ahead of you,' he says, 'and I'm looking forward to seeing how you do.' He tips his hat. 'Good day, Miss Mosey. Ladies.' We all wave goodbye as he weaves his way through the crowd towards the liquor tent.

'I think,' Lydia says, draping an arm over my shoulders, 'that the first thing Annie wants to do in this bright future of hers is take us all out for supper.'

'Ooh, yes,' Liz cries. 'Somewhere *fancy*.'

'Oh, very well,' I laugh. 'I guess all the excitement has made me kinda hungry.'

We're just making our way to the gate when Lydia glances behind and gives me a poke in the ribs. 'Looks like we've picked up a stray.'

It's Mr Butler, loaded down with his gun case and fold-up table, hurrying towards us through the crowd. He raises his arm . . . and drops the table with a clatter; Lydia does a poor job of hiding her mirth.

'Excuse me, Miss Mosey?' he calls. 'Would you wait a moment, please?'

'Perhaps he wants a rematch,' Lydia whispers.

'Or something else entirely,' Sarah Ellen adds.

I step away from my distracting sisters and wait for Mr Butler, wondering what he could want.

'Miss Mosey,' he says, a little out of breath. 'I'm glad I caught you.'

'Mr Butler. Are you here to ask for a rematch?'

He gives a wry smile (that I kinda like), puts the gun case and table down and takes off his hat. 'No, Miss. Under no circumstances – not until I polish up my skills some.'

'Your skills ain't nothing to be ashamed of. Besides, you'd already been shooting for an hour and change before I stepped up. You were probably tired.'

'Now, that *is* a generous perspective, to which I'd add the fact that any fatigue I felt was outweighed by you using a rifle against my shotgun.' He shakes his head, and there's that smile again. 'Fact of the matter is, Miss, you beat me fair and square.'

'Well, despite that, I hope it's been a profitable day for you.'

He looks at me for a long moment. 'Oh, there's no doubt about that, Miss Mosey.'

Heat floods my cheeks and those darned butterflies are fluttering around my insides again. I try to cover it by introducing Ma and my sisters. Mr Butler nods politely and asks how they do. Very well, they reply.

'Well,' I say into the widening silence, 'we're on our way out now, Mr Butler, so if there's something you want to ask . . .'

'I've a show tomorrow night at the Gem Theatre,' he says. 'Trick shooting, all sorts. If you ain't busy, I'd be glad to see you there. You'd get to meet my dog. Do you like dogs, Miss Mosey?'

I can feel my sisters' eyes (*especially* Lydia's) boring into my back.

'Sure,' I reply. 'I like dogs well enough.'

'He's called George. George the Wonder Dog, to give him his full title. He's part of my act.' Mr Butler is turning the brim of his hat between his fingers.

Now, I've beaten plenty of men in shooting contests these past few years. Some take it in sanguine enough part, I guess, but most are downright ornery about it. But I've never encountered a man who's conceded defeat with as much humility and good-sportsmanship as Mr Butler. I gotta admit, I'm impressed.

'So, will you come?'

I'm not sure if he heard Ma's meaningful cough and took its hint, but he does hurriedly go on to say, 'My invitation extends to you all, of course.'

I'm about to say 'I'd be happy to' when Lydia appears at my side and takes my arm.

'Well, that is a kind offer, Mr Butler,' she says in her sweetest voice. 'But I'm sure you won't be surprised to learn that my sister's made quite an impression on Cincinnati society, and she has other offers to field.'

I open my mouth to protest but close it again when she squeezes my arm. I guess she knows what she's doing. Oh, but the poor man looks so crestfallen . . .

'I understand, Miss,' he says, still fiddling with his hat. 'And you're right. I ain't at all surprised – Miss Mosey sure does make an impression. And being a travelling trick-shooter whose best friend's a dog, I cannot pretend to be a member of high society. But I can promise an entertaining night for you all.'

'Oh, Mr Butler,' Lydia laughs. '*All* Annie's suitors say that!' Even as I marvel at how easily and well my sister lies, she continues: 'What she desires is someone who'll go the extra mile to *earn* her time and company. Is that something you think you'll be able to do?'

Mr Butler nods. 'I ain't one to back down from a challenge, Miss. If you'd be so kind as to furnish me with your address, I'll get to thinking what I can do to prove myself.'

Lydia takes some notepaper from her bag and scribbles down her address. She turns to me as she hands the note to Mr Butler. 'How's your diary looking tomorrow, Annie, dear? Do you have many appointments?'

'I, er . . . A few, I think . . .'

Liz and Sarah Ellen sidle up on either side of me like a pair of sly cats.

'I believe Captain Price is due to come by for tea,' Sarah Ellen says.

'Oh, wasn't he *handsome*?' Lydia gasps.

'He was,' Liz replies. 'Wealthy too.'

'Not as wealthy as that charming haberdasher . . .'

'Oh yes. Mr Potts, wasn't it?'

'He's due on Wednesday.'

'Quite taken by our Annie, he is.'

'And that *hat* he gave her! Exquisite . . .'

Mr Butler is smiling at me, and I realise my sisters have overplayed their hands. He doesn't believe a darn word they're saying! I smile back to let him know *I* know how ridiculous they're being, and liking very much that he's taking it all in good humour.

'I'd be happy to receive you tomorrow at eleven, if that suits you, Mr Butler,' I say, cutting through my sisters' increasingly fanciful descriptions of my 'suitors'.

'It'll be my pleasure,' he says, before tipping his hat, picking up his cases and disappearing into the crowd.

Ma and I shake our heads as Lydia, Liz and Sarah Ellen descend into gales of laughter.

40

It's probably because I've spent a fair portion of my life worried about where the next meal's coming from, that when there's food to be had, I'll never waste the opportunity to fill my stomach and feel the joy in every mouthful. But this morning, even as Liz and Sarah Ellen place the usual breakfast dishes of scrambled eggs, bacon and cornbread (Lydia makes that specially for me!) on the table, I don't have a mind to eat even a morsel.

'What's the matter, Annie?' Liz asks. 'Not hungry?'

'No, not really.'

Ma, who's sitting next to me, frowns and presses the back of her hand to my forehead. 'What's the matter? Are you feeling ill?'

'No, Ma.'

'Mm, you don't feel hot . . .'

'I'm fine. I'm just a little . . .'

Lydia gives me a cup of coffee and an infuriating smirk. 'Nervous? *Excited*?'

'I'm sure I don't know *what* you mean,' I say, a little huffily.

'She does keep looking at the clock,' Liz says from behind her piled breakfast plate.

'I am not!'

'Yes, you are. I can see your eyes move.'

'Leave your sister alone,' Ma says. 'I'm just relieved she's not sick.'

'Oh, but she is,' Lydia laughs. '*Love*sick!'

'Don't be foolish,' I say. 'I barely know Mr Butler, so how can I have any strong feelings for him?'

'Because he's handsome and well-travelled,' Lydia says.

Liz nods. 'And he's a brilliant marksman.'

'And he's clearly smitten with you,' Sarah Ellen adds.

I spoon some eggs onto my plate, more to make a point than because I'm hungry. 'I'm more interested in his character than any of those things.'

'Most sensible, Phoebe,' Ma murmurs.

'And besides,' I say, narrowing my eyes, 'I have so *many* suitors waiting to call on me. Why should I be nervous about this one?'

We all turn at a scratching noise at the front door.

'What on earth's that?' Lydia strides from the room and a few moments later we hear the door open. 'Why, he*llo* there!' she says. Then, in a louder voice, 'Annie – visitor for you.'

My stomach knots. 'But that can't be Mr Butler, surely? It's only ten-thirty . . .'

'And he didn't strike me as a man who scratches at doors,' Ma says.

Chairs scrape and plates rattle as we all rush to join Lydia. Looking delighted, she stands aside to reveal a large and handsome poodle with white fur and fluffy ears sitting on the doorstep.

'I guess this is Mr Butler's dog, George,' I say, giving him a scratch under the chin.

'Then he must be nearby,' Liz exclaims, and I'm suddenly pushed un-daintily onto the street by my sisters – not the impression I want to make on my one-and-only suitor.

'I can't see him. Can you?'

'No – there are too many people about . . .'

'Girls,' Ma tuts, 'if you'd only behave with a bit more decorum you might notice there's a note tied to this dog's collar.'

'Oh, yes, so there is!'

'It's addressed to Annie.'

'Go on – open it!'

'Well, I'm not going to read it out here . . .'

Back in the breakfast room, accompanied by George and under the eager gaze of my family, I open the envelope.

'What does it *say*?' Lydia says after about two seconds.

'Is it from Mr Butler?' Liz asks, trying to peer over my shoulder.

'Well, of course it is!' Lydia scoffs.

'Actually, it's not,' I smile. 'It's from George.'

'The dog?' Ma says.

'Sure is, and he's got mighty fine handwriting. He says, "Dear Miss Mosey and family, Frank Butler and I cordially invite you to a picnic in Hyde Park. Drink and food provided. Please ask me to *Find Frank*, and follow my lead. Woof woof, George."'

Before I can even consider the fact that I'm being courted for the first time in my life, Lydia's grabbed my hand and is dragging me towards her bedroom. 'Come on, we need to get you ready!'

'What? No! I'm perfectly presentable as I am.'

'Presentable?' Lydia scoffs. 'You're being wooed, Annie. *Presentable* isn't going to cut the mustard.'

'I'm in a dress, ain't I? S'not like I'm planning to ambulate with Mr Butler in nothing but my bare feet and unmentionables.'

'Annie!' Ma cries. 'Don't even *say* such a thing.'

'I'm going as I am, and that's that.'

'Well at least try not to be too . . . airish,' Liz says.

I stick out my chin. 'As I say, he can take or leave me, as he pleases.'

'Hopeless, you are,' Lydia says. 'Can we at least get our hats and things?'

'Sure,' I say, kneeling next to George and stroking his head. 'It won't do any harm to keep Mr Butler waiting a little while.'

*

Good as his word, George leads us right to where Mr Butler's waiting on the corner of Lydia's street.

'He's cutting quite a swell in his Sunday best,' she whispers to me.

'As he should,' Ma adds.

'Fine as cream gravy . . .'

'Hush, Lydia,' I hiss, 'he'll *hear* you.'

She does have a point though; Mr Butler's Sunday best of black pants and frockcoat, deep red waistcoat, silver fob-watch, white shirt with a bowtie, and polished boots is rather fetching. When he sees us, he removes his bowler and smiles right at me.

'Good morning, Miss Mosey,' he says.

'Mr Butler,' I say with a polite nod. 'You remember my mother, Mrs Shaw, and my sisters Mrs Lydia Stein, Miss Liz and Miss Sarah Ellen?'

'Indeed I do,' he beams. 'It's a pleasure to see you all again.'

'Really?' Lydia says, spinning her parasol. 'I'd have thought you'd have wanted our Annie all to yourself.'

'Lydia!' Ma and I hiss.

But Mr Butler doesn't miss a beat. 'Not at all, Mrs Stein.' He taps a handcart with his boot. 'There's too much food here for two.' He gestures up the road towards the park. 'Shall we?'

I walk alongside Mr Butler as he pushes the handcart; Ma and my sisters follow.

Mr Butler nods to George, who's trotting happily at my heel. 'He's taken quite a shine to you.'

'The feeling's mutual. I've never met such a clever dog.'

'Trained him myself. Best performer I ever had. Right, George?'

George barks in reply.

'Where are your people from, Mr Butler?' Ma asks.

'Ireland originally. I came to America when I was thirteen.'

'And have you always been a marksman?'

'No. I've had lots of jobs. Delivered milk in New York City, looked after horses, even went to sea for a spell. Then I took to the stage, first with a dog show, then as a shootist.' He glances over his shoulder. 'I considered myself pretty good, Mrs Shaw – until I competed against your daughter.'

Because he's not looking where he's going, Mr Butler trips and drops the handcart. 'Darn it,' he mutters.

'Here,' I say, taking one of the handles. 'I'll lend you a hand.'

I'm pleasantly aware of his proximity as we share the load all the way to a quiet spot in Hyde Park under the boughs of a buckeye tree. We all *ooh!* and *aah!* when Mr Butler whips off the blanket to reveal china crockery, cheeses, cold meats, sandwiches wrapped in paper, oatcakes, hard boiled eggs, a box of cookies, and even a jar of candies.

We lay everything out on the blanket and settle down in the dappled shade. I choose a spot opposite Mr Butler. I want to observe for a while, get a sense of him. Later I'll ask Ma and my sisters what they think too.

He's made a decent first impression, but I don't put much stock in them. And I sure ain't going all faint and fluttery just because a man's brought me a picnic. I bear scars on my body and in my mind which remind me that perfectly ordinary-looking people can be cruel and violent and, as you know by now, that's made me cautious.

'No beer for you, Mr Butler?' Ma asks as she picks out several bottles of orangeade from the cart.

'No, Ma'am. I don't drink. Might put me off my aim, and then where would I be?'

Ma peers at him suspiciously. 'Perhaps you gamble, then? Or smoke? After all, every man has his weakness.'

We all stare at her; even Lydia looks surprised.

'Ma!' I exclaim. 'You'll be accusing him of being an opium-eater next.'

'Nonsense,' she replies, unabashed. 'I'm just interested in our host.'

'It's all right,' Mr Butler says. 'I work hard for my money and I see no sense in frittering it away on such things. I'd much rather spend it on picnics with new friends.'

'That's all well and good,' Ma continues relentlessly, and in a way that makes me want to curl up and die, 'but if you don't drink, smoke or gamble, then what *is* your vice?'

We're all looking at Mr Butler now, and although I feel

terrible for him, I would like to hear his answer. I just wish Ma wasn't so darn blunt in the asking . . .

Mr Butler nods thoughtfully. 'Well, I don't think this counts as a vice, more of a frivolity really.' We all lean closer. 'I write poetry.'

'*Really?*' Lydia exclaims a little too loudly to be considered polite.

'Really,' Mr Butler says.

'What sort of poetry?' I ask.

'Poems about life on the road, I bet,' Liz says.

'Yes,' Lydia nods. 'Shooting, hunting, manly pursuits.'

'No,' Mr Butler says. 'I mostly write romantic poems.' He gives us a bashful smile. 'I guess I'm quite sentimental at heart.'

He speaks with such sincerity that even Ma seems mollified. 'Well,' she says. 'I wasn't expecting *that*.'

None of us were, and once again I find myself pleasantly surprised by Mr Butler.

We eat, drink and enjoy the sun. Mr Butler graciously answers lots of questions (mostly from Lydia) about his travels around America, his stage show, his love of animals and memories of Ireland.

When Lydia runs out of questions, he turns to me. 'Actually, Miss Mosey, as a fellow nature lover, would you accompany me to the pond? There's something there that might interest you.'

Ignoring my sister's smirks, I say, 'I'd be happy to,' get up, dust off the crumbs and take Mr Butler's proffered arm.

'So, have you travelled much, Miss Mosey?'

'No, though I'd like to go farther afield one day. I hear so much about the big eastern cities, and I'd love to see mountains. Ohio's so flat.'

'Well, there are mountains to the east of this state, but you ain't seen nothing until you've been to the Rockies. Jagged peaks capped with snow, endless green forests and lakes of polished silver.'

'Why, Mr Butler, you really *are* a poet!'

'I could write one for you, if you like?'

'I suppose you could,' I laugh. 'Although I have no idea what you could say.'

We stop by the pond. It's covered with lily pads and flecks of sunlight, but it's nothing special, s'far as I can see.

'So, what is it you wanted to show me?' I ask.

'Ah, well, to be honest, I just wanted to have some time alone with you. I hope you don't mind?'

As a matter of fact, I don't. I've seen and heard enough to allow Mr Butler a little bit closer, so I say, 'Why don't you call me Annie from now on?'

Mr Butler's smile stirs up those butterflies again. 'And please – *Annie* – call me Frank.'

PART FOUR

41

WINTER 1877

I'm a good enough reader now to have fallen in love with dime novels. They've got names like *Blood Canyon, Smoke Wagon,* and *A Thief's End* and they're full of tales from the Wild West: of camping under the stars, of lawmen and bandits, prospectors and thieves, gunfights, possees and poker games that always end with flying lead and broken glass.

They're supposed to be true – Mr Katzenberger swears they are – but I reckon some scribblers exaggerate to make their stories more sensational. They feature real life people though – like gunfighter Wild Bill Hickock, famous frontiersman William 'Buffalo Bill' Cody, and (my favourite), bootlegger and horse-thief, Belle Starr.

Anyway, sometimes these dime novels have a romance part, where the hero falls in love. Those parts always slow the story down, s'far as I'm concerned and I always skip ahead to the next fistfight, robbery or act of black betrayal. So, I ain't going to go on and on about the parts of my life that might make folk fall asleep.

I'll just say this: over the course of the next few months

Frank became a regular visitor, and changed from being my suitor to being my spark. We spent many fine days hacking about the countryside with George and either Ma, Liz or Lydia as chaperones, and returning to play cards and talk into the evening. He taught me how to shoot a pistol (as good a way to my heart as any I can think of) and over time I learned that Frank is a generous and kind-hearted man more than worthy of my affection.

He fell for me the moment he saw me looking up at him at the fair, or so he says, anyway. Such mutual affection is not to be taken for granted, and we married in Greenville, with Ma and my sisters' approval (they adore Frank nearly as much as I). Everyone was there – Mr Katzenberger, the Edingtons, Huldie and the Fairheads, and the many friends I've made during my shooting contests. It was such a happy day!

Frank warned me that life on the road as a trick shootist is hard: living hand-to-mouth, roaming roads and riding rails to travel state to state, city to city, town to town, taking part in competitions during the day and performing his act in theatres at night. He said he'd understand if I didn't want to accompany him on his endless odysseys around America.

'Let's get one thing straight,' I told him. 'I won't be left behind in Ohio. No, sir! A husband and wife should be together. Besides, I want an adventure.'

And so, six months after our wedding and hundreds of miles down the road, I find myself sitting by the window in a cheap hotel room situated in the backstreets of Richmond, Virginia, with George lying across my feet, the photograph of Ma, Pa and me by the bed, and John's whittled turkey in my hand.

It's about ten in the morning, but Frank was tuckered out when we arrived last night so he's sleeping in. I don't mind – there's plenty to look at on the narrow street below. Boisterous gangs of stevedores trudging to the docks for another hard shift loading up boats. Pawn shops with dusty windows, run-down pharmacies, mean-looking saloons and bit-houses. This is the tenderloin, a pretty rough part of town, but it's all we can afford.

Sure seems like the big cities ain't free of the grinding poverty we have in such sad abundance in the country. A ragged beggar, face lost behind a tangled beard, shuffles along, totally ignored, with his hand out. From here I can also see the Capitol Building shining on top of its hill; I wonder if the politicians, movers and shakers up there know – or even care – about the plight of this fellow and the many others like him?

Another, wearing a tattered grey Confederate soldier's jacket sleeps propped up in a doorway. A broken veteran of the losing side of the Civil War, he has no legs, just stumps that end well above the knees; his pant hems are pinned to his belt; his slouch hat lies upturned on the ground in front of him.

A middle-aged black man with a newspaper tucked under his arm slows down then stops in front of the legless soldier. His face is unreadable as he dips a hand into his pocket, tosses a coin into the hat and walks on.

The irony of a man who not long ago was enslaved giving alms to one who fought on the side that wanted to keep him in chains ain't lost on me, and I wonder what would have happened if the soldier had awoken and seen the face of his benefactor. Would he have been grateful? Angry? Humiliated? Guess I'll never know. Just like how I'll never know how one human being can hold malice and despisement against another just because of the colour of their skin.

Time passes. I reach down and give George a scratch behind his ears.

I'm getting used to this new life of never stopping in one place for long, and not knowing what the next day will bring. It's an adventure, all right, and made especially so because I've become Frank's assistant. On stage, I load his guns and hold out his targets; I was nervous at first, although not as much as Frank, who was terrified of hitting me!

To be candid, despite the quality of our act and how hard we work, we're only just scraping by. What we earn barely covers our travel, accommodation, food and ammunition. On top of that we have to keep our togs and mud-pipes clean (although I do the mending and decorating myself), and ensure dear George is fed and looked after.

Course, I'm used to scraping by with nothing but lint in my pockets, but it's especially nerve-wracking when you're *itinerant* poor; at the cabin we always had a roof over our heads and wood for the fire; if we go bust out here we'll be on the streets at the mercy of gully washers and road agents.

A moan comes from the bed. Frank rolls over and I'm horrified to see that his face is sweat-slick and has the hue of a dead fish.

'Frank, what's wrong? You look *terrible*.'

'Thanks,' he gasps. 'I feel worse. I think it was those oysters . . .'

I jump aside as he clamps a hand over his mouth and hurls himself towards the washbasin . . . and only just in time. I rub his back as he retches up last night's supper. When finished, he collapses onto the bed.

'Oh, my guts . . .' he moans. 'Are you well? You ate them too.'

'I only had one – I thought them slimy. But listen, you can't perform in this state. I'll go to the theatre, explain you're sick—'

'Hold your horses, Annie. I made an agreement, and I'm damned if I'm going to let a bad oyster make me go back on my word.'

'That's your pride talking. You can hardly stand up, let alone shoot.'

Frank gives a mere ghost of his usual smile. 'I'll be fine by tonight. I just need to rest.'

Evening's come and Frank still looks sick. I washed him and sat with him as he sweated and shook, then headed out to get some plain crackers, leaving George to look after him. The few he ate he's kept down, which I'm taking as a good omen, but he's still green around the edges.

'Sun's setting,' I say. 'You still want to go?'

'Got to. We're nearly out of tin.' Frank swings his legs out of the bed and sits, head lowered, gripping the sheets in both hands. 'Besides, I ain't thrown up in a while.'

'That's because you ain't eaten.'

'I'm still going.'

'Well, all right then . . .'

'We'd better leave George behind. I don't want to risk the apple trick tonight.'

As I help Frank dress, he says, 'How you feeling about our great adventure now?'

I finish knotting his tie, stand on tiptoes and kiss him. 'I am having a wonderful time.'

'You sure?'

'Sure as a gun.'

We gather our cases, say goodbye to George and head out into a cool Richmond night. Our breath mists as we make our way through crowded streets towards the Bella Union

Theatre; Frank's performed there before and knows the way. Jaunty piano music and raucous laughter drift from the saloons (which are probably filled with the stevedores I saw this morning) and the streets are alive with pleasure-seekers.

'Here we are,' Frank says, sounding out of breath. 'Third Street and Clay. It's down here.'

We head down a narrow road lined with tenements. Ahead is a larger building that was once white but is now a dirty grey; it looks like a pretty mean and run-down place.

Frank leads me down the side of the theatre, through the stage door and into a dingy room with steps at the far end leading up to the stage. This is backstage, where the acts wait for their turn to perform. And such performers they are! Jugglers with twirling batons, burlesque dancers dressed in black lace and ostrich feathers, a couple with a dog act surrounded by sheepdogs, a trio of singers practising scales, and a near-naked firebreather stinking of alcohol.

Frank points through the throng at an ornery-looking man of about fifty with long greasy hair parted down the middle. He's waving a finger under the nose of a younger man wearing a bright chequered suit and round-rimmer hat.

'That's Mr Bennett, the theatre manager who booked me.' Frank shakes his head. 'He's so mean, he'd steal a fly from a blind spider.'

'And the other?'

'His compere.' Frank dabs his brow. 'Come on, let's go rescue the poor fellow.'

'You're supposed to gee the crowd up, raise their mood,' Mr Bennett growls, still brandishing his finger like a pistol. 'Entice 'em back again tomorrow, on the promise of an uproarious time unmatched by any of our rival establishments.'

'But they're so drunk they don't listen to a word I say,' the compere sighs.

'Then shout louder. And be *funnier*, goddammit! And for Christ's sake, no more jokes about Abe Lincoln. Those that loved him get sore being reminded that he's dead, and those that hated him revel in the fact. It creates rancour and disorder, and I don't need that in my joint.'

'Nor me,' the compere mutters. 'It makes them throw things.'

'Mr Bennett?' Frank says.

'Yeah?' he replies, dismissing the compere with a wave. 'Frank, is it? The shootist?'

'That's me. And this is my wife and assistant, Mrs Butler.'

Mr Bennett gives me the briefest of nods and turns his shrewd eyes back to Frank. 'You look like hell, son.'

'I'm all right,' Frank says stoutly.

'You'd better be, because you're about the only decent act I got tonight and the crowd's getting rowdy. You're on after the most godawful acrobat troupe I ever saw. I got ten bucks on at least one of 'em breaking their neck tonight. The compere'll give you the nod.' He clomps off. 'Come see me about payment when you're done.'

From the wing we watch an acrobat team use chairs and each other to form human towers and pyramids. Some look way too old for this sort of thing, and one actually loses his balance and tips over his chair into the front row. The crowd roars with laughter and one beef-headed drunk even keeps a hold of the poor acrobat's pants to stop him getting back onstage. I see the compere in the shadows, taking a sip from a flask and wincing.

What a place . . .

My green-tinged husband's leaning against the wall. 'We need to change the act.' He holds out a shaking hand. 'I ain't steady enough to shoot anything from your hand, so we'll stick to glass balls and candles.'

'All right.'

'We'll be fine s'long as I don't puke on the front row.'

We wait as the acrobats hurry from the stage, followed by catcalls and jeers from the crowd. The compere sidles up. 'You're next. Wait here while I introduce you.'

Frank takes his shotgun and six-shooters from the gun case as the compere runs through his patter (barely audible over the crowd), then we stride onstage to confront a sea of ruddy-cheeked and boozy faces. It's hot, close and intimidating, and the stink of sweat, spilt beer and tobacco smoke is overwhelming.

As Frank steps to the front of the stage and begins his usual speech, I lay the glass balls, candles and playing cards we'll be using for the show on the table.

'. . . and so, without further ado, allow me to astonish you with my unerring aim and shooting skills!' Frank goes to the far side of the stage. He looks unsteady and my nerves get worse; this is not a crowd we want to disappoint.

I toss a glass ball into the air. Frank raises his shotgun, fires (the sound is so loud indoors) . . . and misses. I manage to catch the ball and I throw it again. Another shot, another miss, and this time the ball shatters on the floor in a sad little puff of feathers.

Frank gives the jeering crowd a sickly smile. 'Just getting my eye in.' He nods and I throw another ball. He hits this one and the air fills with white powder. There are a few ironic cheers. Another ball, another miss. Oh Lord . . . Mr Bennett's watching from the back of the auditorium, and I just want to grab poor Frank and drag him off the stage. I know we need the tin, but really . . .

Then, from out of the boos, catcalls and unsavoury language someone shouts, 'Let the girl shoot!'

42

'Yeah! She might be able to hit something!'

'*Gotta* be better than this fella!'

'Ha! A monkey could shoot straighter!'

This is awful. Frank's swaying on his feet. I rush over to stop him falling.

'Let's just go,' I hiss, 'before this lot turn ugly.'

'We need the money.'

'I know, dear, but Mr Bennet's not going to pony up for this.'

Frank shakes his head as if trying to clear it, then says, 'You do the shooting.'

I stare at him. 'Me?'

'Sure. You know the act and you ain't about to keel over.' Frank gives me a wry smile. 'And listen, it's what *they* all want to see.'

Now, I've shot in front of audiences for years, ever since Mr Katzenberger took me to my first turkey shoot. But my time on the road with Frank has shown me that a trick-shooting act is different. It ain't just about hitting targets.

You have to talk to the audience, get 'em to like you. *Entertain them.*

'I don't know about this . . .'

Frank presses the shotgun into my hands. 'Go on now. You can do it. All you need to be is . . . you.'

'Well,' I say, taking the gun. 'All right then.'

There's no time to prepare. No time to even think. I just walk on wobbly pins up to the front of the stage and drop a curtsey. The crowd quietens; perhaps they weren't expecting me to take up their challenge.

'Witness a good man brought down by a bad oyster,' I cry, hoping my voice carries to the back. 'But the show must go on. And so, by popular request' – I point to the man who called on me to perform – 'I'm takin' over.'

The whole place erupts in cheers and the thunder of two hundred feet thumping on the ground. An encouraging start, I guess. I examine the shotgun as if I've never seen such a thing before, and say, 'Now, which is the end that goes bang?'

The crowd laugh and don't throw anything. Frank's ready by the table. I skip to my mark and tap my finger three times on the shotgun barrel; Frank picks up three glass balls.

'Thin end's the noisy one!'

I glance at the shouter and freeze. He's clearly slewed and is sporting a dead-eyed, belligerent expression that reminds me of *him*, and whenever I think of *him* my body reacts in a way I've grown to hate: my heart pounds, my brain scrambles, my hands shake.

I take a breath.

It ain't him.

I take another.

Annie. It ain't him.

And another.

Goddamit, it . . . ain't . . . him.

At last ready to buckle to my task, I set my legs apart so I'm nice and balanced and nod to Frank. He tosses the glass balls. It's dark in here for shooting, but the glass shines obligingly. *Squeeze, bang, rack. Squeeze, bang, rack. Squeeze, bang, rack.* Three shattered glass balls, three explosions of dyed feathers, and one mightily impressed crowd.

'Well, heck,' I cry to the shouter, who's now clapping harder than anyone. 'So it is!'

Show's over, this most difficult of crowds has been satisfied, and the fee will pay for tonight's hotel room. I've left a relieved Frank outside to get some air while I go find Mr Bennett.

The next act's onstage: a large lady packed into a fading silk dress singing bawdy songs. Her huge voice echoes down the narrow, damp-smelling corridors, as do all the wrong notes her pianist hits. The crowd sounds unsettled and rowdy again, but they're not my problem any more. I spy a door next to a broom cupboard marked 'Manager', and I give it a knock.

'Whaaat?'

Sounds like Mr Bennett's mood ain't improved. I open the door and find him in a tiny office, squeezed behind a desk chomping an unlit cigar and counting greasy dollar bills. He squints up at me. 'Who are you?'

'I'm Mrs Butler. We met earlier.'

'Ah, yeah,' he says, putting the money in a metal box. 'Mrs Frank Butler.'

'I've come for our payment.'

'Have you now?' He keeps his beady eyes on me as he lights the cigar, puffing hard on the wet end. 'Well, I watched his act. And as I watched, I thought to myself, that's strange, I was sure I'd booked a *sharp*shooter.'

I grit my teeth. 'Now Frank'd be the first to admit he had a bad night—'

'It's been a bad night, all right. You hear that racket out there? The drunkest piana player in Virginia?'

'I—'

'Well I do, and I'll be hearing it in my nightmares tonight. Frank was the only decent act on the bill, and he blew it. Goddam embarrassment.'

My hackles are *bristling*, but I think of the money and how much we need it. 'I took over, shot every target and left your audience happy.'

'So?'

'So, I want what's owed.'

'But I booked Frank Butler, not his wife.' He locks his cash box. 'Meaning I don't owe you a red cent.'

'You're *bilking* us?'

'Why should I pay a performer I didn't book?'

I glare at him, wishing I had Frank's Model 3 to brandish. 'Frank told me I'd have to deal with chisellers and conmen if I came out on the road. And here you skulk, taking any opportunity to cheat tin from honest hardworking folk.'

Mr Bennet stands. He towers over me. 'You want to watch your tone when you talk to me in my own place.' His voice is low and dangerous. 'Now git, or you won't be playing at the Bella Union again.'

Faced with a threatening man makes me think of *him* again – but this time I quash the feelings before they freeze me up. I'm not an afeared little girl any more, I'm a young woman, a crack shot with a strong body and independent mind. Mr Bennett, for all his size and bluster, don't scare me one bit.

'On any other day my Frank's the best darn shot in America. And with me by his side we're the best darn double-act too.' I wave my finger under his bloodshot nose. 'And I promise you this, Mr *Bennett*, we ain't ever stepping foot in your fleapit again. You can make do with acrobats who can't balance, singers who can't hold a note, and liquored-up piano players.

You're the one who's blown it, all for the sake of five lousy dollars.'

And I storm out, slamming the door behind me.

I find Frank outside and I'm glad to see there's a bit more colour in his cheeks.

'You look furious.' He smiles. 'Let me guess, Bennett didn't pay up.'

'Said he'd booked you, not your wife.'

Franks wraps his arms around me. 'Did you shoot him?'

'Didn't have my gun.'

'Oh well, never mind, Annie. We'll get him next time.'

'Gave him a piece of my mind though.'

'I bet.'

I sigh. 'We're nearly out of money. How are we going to pay for our room?'

'Well, it seems my luck's changed. Some of the lushes saw me on their way out. Said they'd never seen anything like you before and asked when you'd be back so they could catch the next show.'

'That's nice, I guess.'

'Gave me a couple-a bucks too.'

I breathe a sigh of relief. 'Well, that's tonight's board sorted anyways.'

'And tomorrow can look after itself.' Franks grins. 'Now, I think you and me need to discuss my act, and think about making it *our* act.'

43

FALL 1878

'What do you think of Oakley?'

Frank looks up from cleaning my Peacemaker. 'For what?'

'My stage name. Annie Oakley.'

He thinks for a moment. 'What's wrong with Butler? Or Mosey, for that matter?'

'Because they're my real names. My day-to-day names. I'm a different person on stage, so it seems right to have a different name for her.'

'Makes sense, I guess.' Frank puts the gun back in its case and closes the lid. 'But why Oakley?'

'You of all people should know *that*,' I say, firing him my best frown. 'It's after the neighbourhood in—'

'Cincinnati where we first met,' Frank grins. 'Course I know.'

'Hmm,' I say, settling back down in my chair.

'Annie Oakley it is, then. I'll get the posters changed in the morning.'

We're in our dressing room at the Lysander Theatre in St Paul, Minnesota. We finished our act a half hour ago but there's no hurry to leave – we're performing here for two more nights so the room's ours to cool our heels in for now. They've even provided a big cushion for George.

Times are still tough, and this is the first well-paying job we've had for months; how Frank sweet-talked the proprietor into getting us on the bill, I'll never know. But anyways, we'll be back on the long hard road again soon and still without ten bucks to our name. We're hankering for a permanent gig, something secure. A circus, maybe – but only if they treat their animals right.

'I can't remember ever feeling so tired,' I say, closing my eyes and yawning.

'Well, you didn't seem so on stage.'

'That, my dear, is because I'm a professional from top to bottom.'

'Good crowd tonight.'

I open one eye. 'They weren't drunk like normal, s'what you mean.'

There's a knock on the door and one of the young theatre runners pokes his head inside. 'Message for Mrs Butler,' he says, handing me a piece of paper. 'I'm to wait for a reply.'

I read, then reread the note. 'It's from Chief Sitting Bull.'

'Sitting Bull?' Frank exclaims. '*The* Sitting Bull? Of the Battle of Little Bighorn?'

We both turn to the runner.

'The very same,' he replies. 'He's right here in the theatre. Watched the show. Watched *you*.'

'But I thought he was under arrest in Fort Yates,' Frank says.

'He's been given special permission to tour the States,' the runner says. 'Tonight's his first public appearance.'

Frank blows out his cheeks. 'So, what does he want?'

'He's requesting a photograph be taken of me and him together,' I murmur. 'He's offering sixty-five dollars.'

'Sixty-five dollars?' Frank says. 'That'll come in handy.'

'Oh, Frank! I'm not accepting sixty-five dollars just for a photo. That's daylight robbery.'

'But he's *offering* . . .'

'No. Absolutely not.'

'So, what message shall I take back?' the runner asks.

'No message,' I say, standing up, smoothing down my dress and putting on my hat. 'You can take me instead.'

The runner leads me upstairs to a quiet part of the theatre where a smartly dressed middle-aged man with a thick grey beard is waiting outside a door. He looks surprised but pleased when he sees me.

'Mrs Butler,' he says. 'I see you got my note.'

'Your note?'

'Well, not *my* note, just my writing. The words are Chief Sitting Bull's, dictated to me and delivered to you.' He smiles. 'My name is Alvaren Allen, Chief Sitting Bull's travelling companion and business manager. I've convinced our government to temporarily release him to undergo a tour of Canada and the northern states of America – under guard, of course. I've called it The Sitting Bull Connection.'

'I see. And what does he do on this tour?'

'Well, he doesn't really do anything. Sitting Bull's notoriety is enough to generate considerable public interest. There's no one in America who wouldn't pay to see the man who defeated General Custer at the Battle of Little Bighorn.' He laughs. 'And yet the only person *he* wants to see is *you!*'

'But why?'

'Let me tell you something, Mrs Butler. Sitting Bull *endured* the show tonight. He sat through the whole thing stony-faced. Seemed to me his mind was speculating on things a long way away.' He raises a finger. 'Until, that is, you tripped on stage. He leaned forward and watched every shot you made. You've a remarkable gift, and he sure appreciated it. Asked me to send you a message as soon as the curtain dropped.'

'Well, I'm flattered, but I won't take his money. I would be pleased to meet him though.'

'And I'd be pleased to introduce you.' Mr Allen knocks on the door, opens it and ushers me into a comfortable, oil lamp-lit sitting-room.

A tall, well-built Indian man of about forty-five stands in the middle of the room, and I've a strong feeling he's been waiting patiently in that position for me to arrive. He's dressed quite simply in a pale blue shirt, animal hide leggings and moccasins. Straight black hair, parted in the centre and decorated with a pair of eagle feathers, falls in two braids that reach down to his waist.

I believe that even if I had no knowledge of Sitting Bull and his years-long campaign leading the Plains Indians' fight against the American government, one look at his deep brown eyes, high and broad cheekbones, stern mouth and prominent nose would tell me that this is a man of importance and character.

'Mrs Butler,' Mr Allen says, 'may I present Chief Sitting Bull, leader of the Hunkpapa Lakota tribe.'

I hold out my hand. 'I'm pleased to meet you, Chief Sitting Bull,' I say as graciously as I can.

'The pleasure is mine, Mrs Butler,' and his warm hand encloses mine.

'Well,' Mr Allen says, 'I'll leave you to get acquainted.'

Sitting Bull sets out a couple of chairs so they face each other, and waits for me to sit before he does so himself.

I take off my hat and place it on my lap. 'Well, I must say, sir, your note came as quite the surprise.'

He inclines his head. 'A fair exchange then. Your act was a surprise to me.'

'Oh, well, I'm glad you enjoyed it.'

'Mrs Butler. My eyes may have been open for the jugglers, acrobats and singers, but I was not watching. But when you demonstrated your skills – ah – *then* I took notice. Understand, my people are warriors. *I* am a warrior, and I have fought many times against rival tribes as well as the white man. During those exchanges I saw many great marksmen, among my allies and enemies. And yet, I have never seen one blessed with as much skill with a gun as you.'

'Well, I don't know about that,' I say. 'My pa taught me when I was young, and I've been shooting ever since.'

Sitting Bull shakes his head. 'There is more to your skills than practice. As I watched you perform your feats with such ease, I realized this woman might be blessed by the Great Spirit. I must meet her, I thought, to see if it's true.'

'And now that you've met me?' I ask, guessing that the Great Spirit is the same to Sitting Bull as the Christian God I believe in is to me.

'Now that I have met you, I know it to be true.'

'Then I thank the Great Spirit, because without his blessing I wouldn't have been able to feed my family, wouldn't have met my husband, and I wouldn't be sitting with you now, Sitting Bull.'

'Sitting Bull.' He leans back in his chair. 'That is the name the white man gave me. It is not my *real* name.'

'Oh. Would you tell me about your real name? I'd like to know.'

'I can,' he says with a glint in his eye. 'But I warn you, this might be a longer tale than you're expecting. When I was born, my father called me Ȟoká Psíče, which means Jumping

Badger. Then, when I was fourteen, I took part in a raid on a Crow settlement and my father was so pleased with the courage I showed he held a great feast afterwards and renamed me Tȟatȟáŋka Íyotake. Which means "buffalo who sets himself to watch over the herd".'

'Buffalo who sets himself to watch over the herd . . .' I murmur. 'Like a protector.'

'Yes. And that is what I have tried to be to my people my whole life.' He pauses, lost in thought, and I see something stir behind his eyes. Sadness. Or anger. Perhaps both. 'Tell me, have you ever been to Dakota?'

'I'm afraid not. This is as far west as I have ever been, Tȟatȟáŋka Íyotake.' (I try my best to pronounce his name properly, and I sure hope I got it right.)

'Dakota is my homeland. You must visit. I think you will like it. Take a horse. You'll never feel as free as when you ride across the open plains of Dakota Territory under the wide blue sky.'

'It sounds beautiful. Do you think you'll ever return?'

Tȟatȟáŋka Íyotake shakes his head. 'No. I am a prisoner. Your government will not let me go. The Indian Wars are over, and they want to keep watch over me to ensure I don't cause them more trouble. All I can do now is look after my family and those of my tribe who stand with me.'

We talk for a long time, Tȟatȟáŋka Íyotake and I. He tells me of his love of horses, his daughters, the ritual of the sun dance. I tell him about my life on the road, my home in Ohio, and how I would miss it if I wasn't allowed to return.

'Being apart from family is hard,' Tȟatȟáŋka Íyotake agrees. 'But I can see the life you have chosen suits you, and I believe you'll travel many thousands of miles and see many places before you settle down.'

'I sure am happy seeing what the world has to offer a poor girl from Ohio.'

'I fear Mr Allen will return soon to fetch me,' Tȟatȟáŋka Íyotake says. 'Before that happens, I have three things to give you.' He produces a pair of leather moccasins, beautifully decorated with tassels, and places them onto my lap. 'My daughter made these before she died. I wore them on the day of the Battle of the Greasy Grass – or Little Bighorn, as you know it. I want you to have them, because you remind me of her.'

I stare at them, hardly knowing what to say. 'I can't take these, they must be so precious to you.'

'They are, and that is why I want you to have them.'

'But I have nothing to give you in return . . .'

'You've given me courtesy, respect' – he leans forward – 'and precious time away from Mr Allen, which is gift enough.'

'Well, I'm glad to be of *some* service,' I smile.

'And now, some advice, from one performer to another. Have you heard of a man called Buffalo Bill?'

'William Cody?' I exclaim. 'Of course! I've read lots of

dime novels about him when he was a gold prospector and Pony Express rider.'

Tȟatȟáŋka Íyotake nods. 'Yes. He's had many jobs. Including fighting Plains Indians with the United States Army and killing thousands of buffalo to feed the men who built the railroads.' He gives me a shrewd look. 'Things you surely also know but thought best not to mention.'

I open my mouth to speak (he's right – I *do* know those things about Mr Cody) but he holds up his hand. 'It's all right, Mrs Butler. I appreciate your tact. And for what it's worth, those days are behind him now. What I wanted to tell you is that he's created a travelling show. It's called the Wild West, and it's in St Paul now.'

'A show? You mean a circus?'

'No . . . More of a demonstration of life on the Western Frontier – a version of it, anyway – with cowboys, rodeo riders, even Plains Indians. He approached me to join, but the time is not right. But you, an expert markswoman with the blessing of the Great Spirit? Seek out Mr Cody. Ask for a chance to prove what you can do.'

'That does sound intriguing,' I say, chewing this advice and liking the flavour. 'I will.'

There's a knock on the door and Mr Allen pokes his head in. 'Sorry to interrupt,' he says. 'But it's time for us to go back to the hotel. Chief Sitting Bull has a long day tomorrow.'

Tȟatȟáŋka Íyotake nods and waits for Mr Allen to retreat.

'And finally,' he says to me, 'I want to give you a new name. From now on, I shall call you Watanya Cicilia.'

'Watanya Cicilia,' I repeat. 'I like how that sounds. What does it mean?'

The chair creaks as Tȟatȟáŋka Íyotake stands up. He places both hands on my shoulders and says, 'Little Sure Shot.'

44

It's early afternoon and I'm on my way to see the Wild West show. I told Frank about Sitting Bull's advice to seek work with Mr Cody and he agreed it was worth a shot, but I wasn't to get my hopes up. (Frank's at the printers getting my new names added to our advertising posters. *Little Sure Shot*. Who could wish for a better name, or a better man to have bestowed it? However, that expense has pretty much cleaned us out, and neither of us have eaten properly for days.)

My allotted plan is to see the show, and if it's up our street to try and get an audience with Mr Cody and impress upon him the sound business sense it would make to employ me. I know I might be barking at a knot, but I have to try.

I figured (as I lay sleepless in bed last night) that a good way to make a decent impression on Mr Cody is to wear one of my shooting-act outfits. So I've picked out my favourite pleated blue dress with embroidered wild roses up the side, pearl-buttoned leggings, and my wide-brimmed hat with the silver star pin.

There are posters for the show all over the city: pasted to walls, stuck up in shop windows and plastered onto billboards. Heck, there's even a banner strung across Central (and that's a mighty wide street). Mr Cody sure knows how to advertise! I stop to examine a poster nailed to a lamppost. At the top, in bold red letters, it reads:

Buffalo Bill's Wild West

A visit to the American Frontier for 50 cents

Beneath is a picture of the great man himself. With his handsome face and long hair flowing from beneath a cattleman's hat with rolled brim, he looks just the same as on the covers of the dime novels he stars in that I love so much. He's looking out in a sideways direction, and I imagine he's gazing over the rolling plains of the untamed West and about to embark on another thrilling adventure. There's a label below his picture:

COLONEL W F 'BUFFALO BILL' CODY,
FAMED SCOUT, HUNTER AND FRONTIERSMAN.

All around him are smaller pictures of American cowboys riding bucking broncos, Mexican vaqueros lassoing steers, Pony Express riders at full gallop and Indians in feathered headdresses attacking a settler's cabin. All scenes taken from the show, I guess. It must be wonderful to be part of such a great and glorious endeavour!

I take the trolley bus out of the city to the park where the Wild West's all set up. There are droves of people (including, pleasingly, lots of children) converging on an open-to-the-sky arena surrounded on three sides by tiers of seats. The fourth side is a huge wooden backdrop painted to look like the snow-capped mountains and scrubby plains of the Wild West. Beyond that sprawls a fenced-off area filled with tents and animal pens. That must be where the performers live.

I join the queue, pay my fifty cents and enter the passage between already packed seats. I find a good spot in the front row, where there's nothing but a low barrier separating me from an arena of hard-packed earth and hoof-trampled grass.

A band of cowboys wearing wide-brimmed hats, black shirts and leather chaps are playing a waltz on clarinets, trombones, tubas and drums, and I'm soon tapping my foot to the beat. It ain't long before every seat's taken – there must be *thousands* of eager spectators here. The clamour fades to an excited murmur when the cowboys strike up a grand old tune that quite stirs my heart. I lean over the barrier, pop a humbug into my mouth (which always reminds me of Pa) and wait with bated breath for the show to begin.

Hoofbeats! Hollers! Then a column of horses and riders bursts from a gate in the backdrop and gallop into the arena.

The air fills with dust and the thunder of hooves. Texan cowboys and Mexican vaqueros whirl lassos over their heads. Indian braves in buckskins and feather war-bonnets brandish carbines. The ground shakes and I'm on my feet, clapping and cheering along with everyone else!

Then, in perfect time, they form up to create an avenue right in front of the backdrop gate. The band strikes up a fanfare as another rider emerges into the sunlight on a beautiful black stallion. The crowd cheers even louder as he canters down the avenue, waving his hat, and draws to a stop right in front of me.

Colonel William 'Buffalo Bill' Cody looks every inch the dashing frontiersman. Tall, straight-backed and comfortable in the saddle, his brown hair loose over his shoulders. He's dressed in a black shirt, tan britches held up with a wide belt, and black leather knee boots.

He gives a bow and speaks in a voice that echoes around the arena. 'Ladies and gentlemen! Allow me to welcome you to the Wild West, featuring *gen-u-ine* American cowboys, Mexican vaqueros and Plains Indians who will demonstrate their skills with horse, steer and firearm, and re-enact exciting events from the frontiers of our great country, all for your entertainment.'

With deafening halloos, shouts and cries, the performers break up and begin a dazzling display of high-speed horsemanship the like of which I ain't *never* seen before.

Indians race each other up and down the arena, piebald horses stretched full-length and skidding to stops in billowing clouds of dust. One brave on horseback races another on foot. They run like greased lighting and have to turn sharp halfway through, which is harder for the horse; the rider wins, but it's closer than you might think. There's so much going on I don't even know where to look!

After the races, dozens of horses are brought into the arena for the cowboys and vaqueros to lasso, ride as bucking broncos, or do laps at speed standing up on the saddle. Lowing Texas Longhorn steers are expertly corralled. Buffalo emerge from the gate with their shaggy heads lowered and legs pounding so hard I feel the ground shake. Mr Cody rides among the action, directing and joining in as he sees fit – a magnet to draw the eye.

'Such big strong fellows, those cowboys,' a woman behind me gushes. 'I much prefer them to the spindle-shanked dudes and tenderfeet we find in the city.'

Finally, the cowboys, vaqueros and braves round up all the livestock and urge them back through the gate, leaving the arena empty. What's next, I wonder?

The band strikes up a jaunty tune as a weather-beaten stagecoach pulled by six horses appears and begins a leisurely tour around the arena. This must be the famous Deadwood Stage. There's three rifle-armed men on the roof, including the driver, and some well-dressed passengers waving at us from inside. The music changes to a more threatening tone as a thirty-strong mounted Indian war band gives chase, whooping and waving their carbines.

The stagecoach driver lashes the reins until the wagon's really cutting some dirt. The crowd gasp and there are screams as the Indians and defenders open fire on each other with pistols and rifles (using blanks, of course). Round and round the arena they fly, shooting, shouting, filling the whole place with gun smoke. One brave actually leaps from his mare onto the wagon roof for some hand-to-hand combat with the driver!

I know it's all acting, but it seems so *real*.

The wagon rattles to a halt in the centre of the arena. The Indians circle on their horses, laying down fire. The music changes thrillingly as Buffalo Bill and a cohort of cowboys emerge from the door and ride down on the attackers. A battle ensues, with cowboys and Indians shooting and shouting and tumbling from their mounts as if they'd bit the dust. Eventually, the attackers are run off and the stagecoach is saved.

It sure is exciting, and the crowd's loving every second – waving their hats and cheering Bill's rescue. And yet I can't help but think of the plight of Thatȟáŋka Íyotake (who I'm proud to call my friend), the Hunkpapa Lakota, and all the Plains Indians – forced to fight the white man, then driven from their homelands, confined to reservations, imprisoned, killed . . .

Mr Cody's set up his Wild West so white folk and Indians work together for a common cause, and I sure do like that approach. But I wonder how these braves feel about performing as villains even though, seems to me, they're the ones who were wronged in the first place. If I get to join, I'll be sure to ask them about it.

And so the show goes on, with more breathtaking riding, lassoing and shooting, until the show ends with a grand parade led by Buffalo Bill. I'm in a kind of happy stupor as they trot through the gate. I know with complete certainty that this is where Frank and I belong: earning a steady income, performing for wonderstruck crowds with a travelling family of the best artistes in the land.

Now I've got to find a way of speaking to the great man and convincing him of the same thing.

45

S'far as I can tell the only way to get into the performers' compound is through that backdrop gate. So, I hop over the barrier, make my way over the arena as unobtrusively as I can and duck on through into a short passage made of strung-up fabric. What I find on the other side makes me gasp.

There are people and animals *everywhere*, going about their business like they're killing rattlers. Stagehands bustle past carrying rope and saddles. Cowboys groom mounts, vaqueros coil lassos, Indians reload carbines. One rodeo rider's having his whiskers shaved by a barber in front of a tent. A group of Indian children scamper past chasing a little dog. Sparks fly as a blacksmith hammers out a horseshoe on an open forge.

A refectory standing tall in the tent village houses a posse of grub-slingers sweating over stoves and dishing up stew to a line of weary performers. There are wagons, boxes, barrels, sacks, hay bales and bundles of cloth lying about all over the place. Further in I find a whole area of pens for the horses, buffalo, cattle, mules, elk and goats. The air rings with shouts, laughter and hoofbeats, and smells of smoke, roasting meat, leather and dung.

I'm about to ask a passing porter where Buffalo Bill might be when I see him looking perfectly at home in the midst of all this chaos, leaning back on his horse with the reins loose between his fingers saying 'Howdy, Trixy' and 'Good show today, Dutch,' and 'Well done, Micah' to folk as they pass.

I work my way through the crowd towards my quarry, sidestepping cowboys leading horses and stagehands wheeling handcarts. I've just about reached Mr Cody when he swings to the ground and hands the reins to a stable hand. 'Give Charlie a brush before you feed him, would you?' he says, then he's off and striding towards a tent set apart from all the rest.

I trot after him. 'Excuse me, Mr Cody? *Sir?*'

He turns and pins me with a gaze that says with some eloquence that he's not pleased to see me. 'Who are you?' he barks. 'You ain't one of mine.'

'That is so, sir—'

'Then what are you doing here? How'd you get in?'

'I came through that gate yonder,' I say. 'I know I may have overstepped the mark by coming in—'

'I'll say you have! This is a private area you've snuck into. I've a good mind to run you off.'

'Please don't do that,' I say, holding out my hands. 'Not yet, anyway. You've every right to be mad at me, but I promise I would never normally trespass like this. It's just I'm that eager to speak to you, Mr Cody, and I didn't know of any other way to make it happen . . .'

'Well, it *ain't* happening! There're proper channels, Miss. If you wanted to speak to me, you should have made an appointment with the show manager, Mr Salsbury.'

'Well, I'm real sorry,' I say, feeling desperate, 'but I didn't realise. All I knew was that you'd be leaving town tomorrow and that I just *had* to speak to you. I have a proposal, you see.'

'A proposal?' Mr Cody shakes his head in disgust. 'You know how many proposals I get every week? Hundreds.'

Sensing my chance slipping away, I march up to him and say, 'Sir, I promise it'll be well worth listening to.' I guess I sound as sincere as I feel because his anger simmers down some.

'D'you see the show?' he asks.

'I sure did,' I say with great earnestness. 'It was the most wonderful thing I ever saw.'

He grunts. 'And did you sneak into that too?'

'No, *sir*. I paid my fifty cents and believe I got a bargain for it.'

'Well, that's something, I guess.' He regards me keenly for a moment then says, 'Missy, this is your lucky day. I'm going to give you five minutes. Come with me.'

Me and my jangling nerves follow him into a spacious tent that's well-appointed with a dark wood desk and chair, a fur-covered bed, a stove topped with a steaming coffee pot, and a full gunrack topped off with a 'Big Fifty' Sharps buffalo rifle that I can hardly tear my eyes from.

Mr Cody tosses his hat so it lands spinning on a hat-stand in the corner and says, 'Your five minutes started thirty seconds ago, so you'd best get on with your pitch.'

I take a deep breath. This is it. Frank and my happiness depends on this next five . . . no, *four* minutes. Perhaps I should've prepared a speech . . .

'My name is Annie Oakley,' I say. 'I'm from Darke County, Ohio, and I've been shooting since I was six-years old when my pa taught me to use his Kentucky long rifle. After he died, I used it to hunt and feed my family. At twelve, I started entering turkey shoots to earn a few dollars.'

Mr Cody settles into his chair, draws out a heavy silver pocket-watch and notes the time. 'Who'd you compete against? Local boys? Farmers?'

'That's right. All grown men, and with better firearms than what I was totin', but I still beat 'em. Had to fight just to be allowed to take part too, on account of my sex.'

'Mmm . . .' Mr Cody looks at me thoughtfully. 'Listen, I don't doubt your achievements. What you've told me sounds highly commendable. But you were competing against amateurs, is my point.' He shrugs. 'I only hire professionals, the very best.'

'Mr Cody,' I say quietly but firmly, 'give me the five minutes you promised, and I will get to that very point.'

He smooths back his hair. 'Go on then,' he sighs. 'I'm listening.'

'I'm obliged to you. When I was sixteen, a business associate suggested I accept a professional sharpshooter's challenge at the Cincinnati Fair. I agreed because I was saving up to buy a Colt Peacemaker, just like the ones you got over in that gunrack.'

Mr Cody nods approvingly.

'So I took my Winchester Yellow Boy onto the field and threw down my challenge in front of a dumbstruck crowd, and not to mention a dumbstruck sharpshooter.'

'A bold play,' Mr Cody said. 'What was the contest?'

'Clay pigeons, sir. And you know what? I'd never shot at 'em before.'

'Is that so?'

'It sure is. But I did not let that fact discourage me. Well, those pigeons flew and I matched that sharpshooter shot for shot until we'd both hit twenty-four each. My opponent? Well, he had no notion *what* was going on! He was perspiring and fidgeting and fretting about being beat by a slip of a girl in front of a big crowd.'

Mr Cody leans forward, his pocket-watch forgotten. 'So? Did you win?'

' 'Course I did!' I laugh. 'And not only that, I won his heart too. We were married within the year.'

'Well, hot damn!' Mr Cody laughs. 'A chest shot, huh?

Quite a day for the man! What's his name? If he's on the circuit, I might know him.'

'He goes by the moniker of Frank Butler.'

'Frank Butler . . . Sure. I've heard of him. A good shot. Uses a dog in his act, if I remember?'

'That's right. George the Wonder Dog.'

Mr Cody pours some coffee. 'So, it's a double act?' he says, handing me a mug.

'Yep. But it's me and George who perform. Frank assists. He's my business manager too.'

'Huh. Well, it's an unorthodox set-up, I guess, but I don't have a problem with that.' He thinks for what feels like an age then says, 'All right, Missy, I'm interested. And it just so happens I've recently parted ways with my champion shooter and I need a replacement. So, how about this? You and Mr Butler meet me at the baseball park at nine tomorrow morning – I'll square it with the owners to let you in – and demonstrate your act. If I judge it good enough, we can discuss terms and sign a contract.' He frowns and shakes his shaggy head. 'I mean, what's a Wild West show without a sharpshooting act, eh?'

46

Frank and I put our cases down on the grass and look around at the deserted baseball field and empty stands.

'Are you sure this is the right place?' Frank asks.

'It must be,' I say. 'They were expecting us at the gate.'

'But there's no one here. Where's Mr Cody?'

'Well, we are a bit early. Come on, let's set everything up while we wait.'

It's an overcast day, and the factory chimneys beyond the baseball ground are pouring more grey into the sky. The scene matches my increasingly glum mood. Could Mr Cody have forgotten our appointment? Was he just stringing me along? No, he didn't strike me as the type to do that. But still – where the heck *is* he?

As Frank heads to the second base mark to set up his gear, I load my Colt Peacemakers, Yellow Boy and the Kentucky long rifle (my heart tells me it's right to use Pa's faithful old gun on this important occasion) and lay them in a row on the pitcher's mound.

'What time is it now?' I call.

'Fifteen past the hour.'

'Huh . . .'

'Well,' he says, 'seeing as we're here, how about we practise some tricks?'

'All right,' I sigh. 'What shall we do?'

'Let's start with glass balls in twos, threes and fours. Then we'll scramble some eggs. And how about we finish up with a tossed dime?'

'Sure. Sounds daisy.'

I roll my shoulders, touch my worn-out boot toes a few times then pick up Yellow Boy. I've used my repeater for so long now it really does feel like a part of me, just like Pa said it should. I take a few deep breaths, plant my feet nice and firm and give my patiently waiting Frank the nod. Straight away he starts tossing glass balls. Cares and worries fly away as I sight down the barrel and shoot them, one after the other.

Frank stops throwing every time I need a reload, and after every reload I change the shoulder I aim from. I shoot fifty and don't miss a one; Mr Cody's missing quite a show.

'Twelve to scramble,' Frank calls, and he tosses a chicken egg high into the air.

I put down Yellow Boy, grab a six-shooter in each hand, extend my right arm nice and straight, sight the egg, squeeze the trigger and watch with satisfaction the orange-splatter explosion. Five more eggs follow. I empty the first Colt and raise the second. Six more eggs, tossed faster this time. But my arms are strong, my eyes sharp and my skills honed to the finest point. Pistol reports echo, smoke drifts, and there are no more eggs to scramble.

Frank holds up a dime and backpedals until he's about fifty paces away. I shift position and wait; this is one of the hardest shots in my act and I don't always succeed.

Even from this distance I see Frank's wrist snap as he flicks the coin with his thumb. I kneel down, retrieve my Kentucky long rifle, nestle it into my shoulder and pull back the hammer. A flash of sunlight on the spinning coin draws my eye. It's beginning its descent. I drop my aim, trusting my instincts to get the angle and timing just right, and pull the trigger.

My pa's old muzzle-loader barks and shoots fire, sparks and smoke. I lower the stock to the ground, stand straight as a soldier on parade and look at Frank. He turns to me with a big smile.

'Got it!' he shouts, trotting over. 'I think you've got that trick nailed.'

'Well, that's something, I guess. Pity Mr Cody weren't here to see it.'

Frank's about to say something when he looks over my shoulder and frowns. 'Who's this coming now?'

I turn and see a neat-bearded gentleman wearing a dark suit and derby hat hurrying towards us.

'Fine! Wonderful! A stellar performance!' he says, waving

his walking cane. 'Tell me, Miss Oakley, have you any photographs posing with your gun? We'll need some for publicity.'

Frank and I stare at him. 'Who . . . ?'

'Nate Salsbury. Pleased to meet you. I'm Mr Cody's business partner and manager of the Wild West. He sends his apologies for not being here – urgent business required his attention – but I have his proxy.'

'Well, I'm pleased to meet you, Mr Salsbury,' I say. 'This is my husband and manager, Frank Butler.'

'Pleasure, pleasure,' Mr Salsbury says, shaking mine and Frank's hand. 'I hope you don't mind, but you'd already started by the time I arrived so I thought I'd stay in the shadows, as it were, and watch from afar.' He shakes his head. 'I must say, that's some of the best shooting I've seen in all my years in show business. It's a done deal, s'far as I'm concerned. So, what do you say? You ready to join the greatest show in America?'

Happiness floods into me, a smile spreads across my face, and as Frank puts his arm around my waist I say, 'Yes, sir. I believe we are.'

47

Frank, George and I still had some engagements to fulfil in Minnesota and so couldn't join the Wild West straight away. Instead, we arranged to reconvene a few weeks later in the town of Kalamazoo, Michigan, to discuss terms and sign a contract. After seeing Mr Salsbury's ecstatic response to my act, Frank is determined to negotiate a handsome fee.

That's all daisy, of course. I'm keen to make a decent living at long last and ensure my family never have to endure the hardships of poverty again. But it ain't just the money that excites me about this new caper. For me, it's also about being *part* of something. Working with interesting folk from all over the country who share a love of adventure and life on the road.

These are the thoughts crowding my mind as the train pulls into Kalamazoo station under a bright blue sky and the three of us disembark onto the platform. We'd written to Mr Salsbury telling him which train we'd be arriving on and I'm pleased to see him waving at us from a parked spider phaeton pulled by two white ponies.

'Great, wonderful!' he says, shaking our hands and helping

us stow our cases. 'So good to see you again! Ah, this must be George! Did you have a good journey?'

'It was long,' Frank says, stretching out his back.

'But worth the wait,' I add.

Mr Salsbury urges the horses into a trot. 'Excellent, excellent! Well, the show's being set up outside of town as we speak. The whole crew's looking forward to meeting you.'

'Oh,' I say, feeling a flutter of nerves. 'They know I'm coming then?'

'Well, of course,' Mr Salsbury laughs. 'You're the talk of the camp.'

We clatter down the road into the country where the stands, arena, tent village and animal pens are being set up in much the same way as in St Paul. There are plenty of Kalamazooians milling about trying to peer inside, but it's clear there's to be no performance today.

Mr Salsbury trots us through a gap in the fence, onto the arena floor and draws to a halt in front of the backdrop gate. It's eerily quiet . . .

'All right, then,' he says, extending a hand to help me down. 'You ready, Miss Oakley?'

'Ready, sir?' I ask. 'Ready for what?'

'Why, to meet your new family, of course.'

Mr Salsbury ushers me through the gate and follows behind with Frank and George. When I emerge from the fabric passage, I see the tents and pens set up just the same but there's none of the chaos, bustle and noise from my first visit. Instead, there is a long line of people stretching right down to the other end of the camp: vaqueros and cowboys with their hats in their hands, family groups of Plains Indians, stagehands, stable-hands, porters, cooks, carpenters, blacksmiths ... The whole crew it seems, all quiet and respectful and looking right at me.

I'm so overwhelmed I don't notice Mr Cody until he's right by my side with his arms spread as wide as his smile. 'Miss Oakley,' he booms, 'and Mr Butler. Speaking for myself, Mr Salsbury and everyone you see before you, we are mighty pleased to welcome you to the Wild West.'

Mr Cody walks Frank and me down that long line and introduces us to every person, including the children. 'How do you do?' we say to each other, a sincere greeting that turns strangers into friends-to-be. Some smile and tip their hats. Some nod. Some take my hand and say, 'Welcome, welcome.'

I feel something like a gooseberry stick in my throat as I consider what I believe to be an irrefutable fact: no crowned queen was ever treated with more reverence and respect than I've just been by these whole-souled western folk.

48

It's a sunny Saturday afternoon, exactly two weeks from the day I signed on with the Wild West. I'm about to perform for the very first time and, guided by what must be some kind of divine intervention, it's happening in the same field in Cincinnati where I first met Frank.

I'm pacing around the tent we share. We've got it set up real nice; it even has my name embroidered over the entrance. There's a table and chairs for guests (we love to socialise), cosy beds (one for me and Frank, one for George) a special travelling dresser for my clothes, potted plants, framed photographs, lots of rugs and pillows strewn about and, in pride of place, my own gunrack. Pa's long rifle rests on the top rungs.

I sent word to the whole family, including Huldie and the Fairheads, Mr and Mrs Edington and Mr Katzenberger, inviting them to stay in a nearby hotel (which I covered with my first salary payment) to come see my debut performance.

They arrived in a happy gang yesterday and I took great pleasure showing them the camp and introducing my new friends. They were all a bit tongue-tied (especially Mr

Katzenberger) when Mr Cody came to say howdy. He was so gracious, despite having a mess of things to sort. I think he took quite a shine to John, who's such a cheerful young man now.

Seeing them all looking fit as butcher's dogs did me the world of good (as well as taking my mind off my nervousness). We spent last evening talking and laughing and reminiscing about Pa and Mary Jane, as cowboys sang round their campfires and sparks danced into the sky.

Before we said our goodbyes, Ma drew me to one side. 'Phoebe, do you remember the day you took Pa's rifle and shot that turkey?'

I smiled. 'Sure I do. We had quite the bust up.'

'You were such a little thing,' Ma replied, 'but so determined, so stubborn.'

I took Ma's hands, feeling bones through her paper-thin skin. 'Can't think where I get *those* qualities from.'

'And do you remember what I made you promise that day?'

'That I can go a-hunting and a-traipsing so long as I remain a respectable young woman.'

'Well now, Phoebe, my precious daughter. Seeing you so at home among these upstanding folk, achieving so much acclaim with your shooting and high-spirited nature – and with a fine husband to boot – I'm about the proudest mother in God's great creation.'

Well, I don't need to tell you how much those words mean to me.

The sound of the cowboy band playing up a waltz drifts over the tent roofs, and I can see Mr Cody and his men forming up on their horses near the backdrop gate ready for the welcome parade. I'm not taking part in that because Mr Cody wants my act to be a complete surprise. He said, 'Missy,' – that's his pet name for me – 'they won't know *what* to think when you come out at the top of the show, and still less when they see what you can do with a firearm.'

I'll be out there soon, under the gaze of thousands . . . George, coat brushed to a performance-ready shine, trots over and presses himself against my leg. He wags his tail as I scratch him behind the ears. 'I wish I were as calm and professional as you, honey,' I murmur.

I shake out my arms, pace the tent a few more times then take a repeater from the rack and start to disassemble it. Thing is, I reckon if I was part of that parade I'd get a good sense of the crowd and the arena. As it is, I'll be heading out there cold . . .

Frank, dressed in his best suit, appears in the tent entrance. He sees what I'm doing and says, 'Nervous?'

'Huh?'

'You always strip a shooting-iron when you're nervous.'

'Well, it helps calm me, I guess.' I look down at the gun pieces in my hand and lay them absently on the table. 'Frank?'

'Yeah?'

'What if I foul up? What if I foul up in front of all those people? In front of our new friends? In front of *Bill*?'

'You won't.'

'But how do you know?'

'Because I know *you*.'

The waltz finishes and the band strikes up the tune for the welcome parade, but that's soon drowned out by the noise of hooves and the cheers of the crowd. The Wild West's begun.

49

I trip on through that tunnel, emerge on the other side and head right down the middle of the arena, skipping, smiling and dropping curtseys to all corners.

Good Lord, my heart is *thumping*. There's an ocean of faces looking down at me and they sure don't seem impressed . . . It's dead quiet too; beyond the blood rushing in my ears all I hear are scattered claps and a nonplussed murmur. As for the band's cheerful fanfare welcoming me to the arena . . . Well, it sounds way too loud and out of place in the midst of all this silence.

Who's this little girl? everyone must be thinking (I still look mighty youthful – everyone says so). Well. I'm about to show them.

Our gear's all set up: a table for me with my rifles and shotguns all loaded and laid out in the order I'm going to use them, and boxes of ammo and a blanket laid on the ground. Frank stands ready by a sturdy stool, another table, and a whole mess of straw-filled cases. George sits obediently behind, waiting for his chance to shine.

I skip on over to my table, and just as soon as I pick up Yellow Boy my nervousness fades away like morning mist. I'm in control. I know just what I'm doing.

There are seven soda bottles lined up on Frank's table. I aim and loose off seven shots in quick succession. Gunshots echo. Smoke drifts. There's no cheering or clapping, just silence. Even the band's stopped playing.

I've missed every single bottle.

Just so.

I turn to the audience with a furious frown, stamp my foot, throw off my hat, then lie on my back on the blanket. The crowd murmurs at my antics. Well, there's more to come! Using my elbows and feet for support, I arch my back til it's raised from the ground. Then, by shuffling my feet so they're positioned under my knees, and lifting my arms from the ground, I take my weight on the top of my head. I'm now looking backwards and upside-down at the soda bottles.

I'm utterly focused as I pick up Yellow Boy, press the stock into my shoulder, rack a rimfire and get blazing. In four seconds I've shot off the tops of every bottle and there's soda spraying everywhere.

I leap to my feet, retrieve my hat, and by the time I give a bow the audience is on their feet and turning their disappointed murmur into a cheer of delight. All right. Time to hit 'em again.

I pick up another repeater (a gift from Mr Cody) and nod to Frank, who starts tossing glass balls in the air: one at a time, two at a time, then three, four, five. I swap spent rifles for loaded ones as I go. *Rack, aim, bang; rack, aim, bang; rack, aim, bang,* until we're standing under a huge cloud of multi-coloured powder and drifting feathers.

I put down the last smoking rifle, turn my back to Frank, count three seconds, wheel around, draw my Smith & Wesson from my belt and shoot the last four thrown balls before they hit the ground.

As a pair of stagehands dash up to reload my guns I turn to drop curtseys and bows to the crowd who are now completely enraptured and tearing up Jake with their noise!

Frank's ready, standing on the stool with a playing card held at arm's length. I pick up Yellow Boy, aim, and shoot a hole right through the ace. With a deft flick of his wrist, Frank tosses the card into the air. I track it, shooting four more holes as it tumbles to the ground. Frank picks up the card, holds it aloft, dashes over to the audience and gives it to a delighted little girl.

Then he's back on the stool holding out another card, but this time held side-on; this is one of the hardest tricks for a sharpshooter, and I've lost count of the hours I've spent practising it. Time to see if it was worthwhile . . .

I raise my Colt and extend my arm. I can't see the card so I aim just above Frank's pinched, upturned fingers and snap off a shot. Frank leaps off the stool, picks up the top half of the split card and holds it aloft for the clapping crowd to see.

Frank gives a whistle and George scampers up onto the stool and sits facing me, tongue out, tail wagging. The whole place goes quiet as Frank places an apple on George's head, right between his ears. The band plays a drumroll.

I turn my back and rest a Marlin rifle on my shoulder so the barrel's facing behind me, pointing at George. I take an oval mirror from my pocket, hold it up and angle it so I can see dear, trusting George in the reflection. Then I wrap my thumb around the trigger.

This is the trick that gives me the worst palpitations. George is such a honey, and the thought of hurting him (or worse) is unbearable. (And yet, when I shoot at targets held by my husband, I don't feel any nerves at all!)

I stand steady, and carefully line up the apple. I sense the crowd leaning forward, holding their breaths. I squeeze the trigger. The rifle bucks and the apple explodes into pulp and juice. I run for George, he leaps from the stool, and we meet in the middle to make a great fuss of each other.

The act's nearly over. There's just one more trick to go, the hardest and fastest of them all: eleven glass balls using six different guns in ten seconds. This is the showstopper, the part people will remember, and I'm sure Mr Cody and Mr Salsbury will be watching from somewhere. *Don't mess up now, Annie.*

The stagehands have done their job and I've got a rifle and five double-barrelled shotguns lined up. Frank's back at his table with a fresh box of glass balls at the ready. I give him a nod.

He throws a ball. I pick up the rifle, sight, and shoot. Red powder explodes. By the time I put the rifle back there are two more balls sailing up and glinting in the sunlight. I grab the first shotgun, empty both barrels and add white powder to the red. First shotgun down, next one up. Two more balls, two more bullseyes. Blue powder. Next gun. Yellow powder patters down around me like the softest rain. Down goes that gun, up go the balls. Next gun up – glass shatters – purple blossoms.

Last two. I grab the final firearm. Shoot twice and fill the air with feathers.

It's done. Finished. And I didn't miss a single darn shot.

Frank, with his arm around George, catches my eye, blows out his cheeks, and smiles. I put the shotgun down and give a deep bow to each of the three seating stands. One area on the front row seems especially animated. It's Ma and Lydia and everyone else cheering and clapping and waving their handkerchiefs in the air. Finally, I look up to the heavens and blow a kiss to Pa and Mary Jane.

I back away towards the gate, still bowing to the crowd, as the stagehands rush out to clear away my gear. Frank and George join me just as Mr Cody rides out on Charlie crying,

'Three cheers for Annie Oakley! Three cheers for Little Sure Shot!'

'That went pretty well, I reckon,' Frank shouts over the applause.

'I think so too,' I reply, brain buzzing with new ideas. 'But next time, how 'bout I do some of those trick shots on horseback?'

'I believe if you set your mind to something even as crazy as that, you'll succeed.'

We come out of the tunnel into the camp – *our* camp – and stand aside as the rodeo riders gallop past for the next part of the show. Some tip their hats and say 'Well done, Annie!', and 'Good shootin', Miss Oakley!'

And I know that I'm home.

AFTERWORD

This novel only tells the first part of Annie Oakley's extraordinary life, and the main events I've described are all true: Annie really did learn to shoot to save her family from starvation; she really did suffer terrible abuse at the hands of a couple we only know as the 'Wolves' (I made up the name 'Grace'); she was banned from turkey shoots because she was so darn good at them; she beat Frank Butler and stole his heart at the same time; she really did meet and earn the respect and affection of Chief Sitting Bull, and she charmed and amazed every audience she performed for. Over her many years with Buffalo Bill's Wild West (and, just to be clear, the giant plains-roaming buffalo were actually North American bison) Little Sure Shot thrilled millions of people with her charm and superlative shooting skills. No matter where the show went, or what new and exciting acts Bill and Nate added, it was always Annie who delighted audiences most. They loved her. She was a superstar. And yet, despite the fame and fortune she earned, she remained humble, down-to-earth and generous. (She actually joined Bill later in her life than presented in the book – this change was made to ensure a smoother flow to the story.)

As well as the United States and Canada, Annie also travelled across Europe. She became a star there as well, performing in front of heads of state, and competing against some too. She always won, of course. The highlight of Annie's European travels came when the notoriously reclusive Queen Victoria called her 'A very, very clever little girl' after watching her act.

Just as her ma always wanted, Annie guarded her good name and respectable reputation like a lioness. When newspapers falsely reported that she was a thief and a drug addict, Annie was furious. Every newspaper that refused to retract their lies she took to court, and one by one, Annie won each case. It took years, but to her it was worth the effort.

Something else Annie believed was worth the effort was encouraging women to take up outdoor pursuits and shooting; she had no time for the idea that such things should be the sole domain of men. After all, her own unsurpassed skill and ability to make a good living as a shootist proved that women can do anything men can – so long as they are given the opportunity. 'God intended women to be outside as well as men,' she said. 'And they do not know what they are missing when they stay cooped up inside the house.'

Frank Butler was right by Annie's side throughout all her adventures, all her ups and downs, assisting in her performances and acting as her publicist and manager. When Annie died on November 3rd 1926 at the age of sixty-six, her devoted Frank stopped eating and died eighteen days later. They are buried together in Ohio, not far from where she was born.

But let's not end on such a sad note. Instead, we'll give the last word to Annie – I think she deserves it, don't you?

'Aim at the high mark and you will hit it.
No, not the first time, not the second time and maybe not the third.
But keep on aiming and keep on shooting for only practice will make you perfect.
Finally, you'll hit the bullseye of success.'

ACKNOWLEDGEMENTS

I would like to thank Chloe, my peerless editor at Andersen Press, for all her advice, support, and being patient when I kept asking for more time to finish the first draft. I'm sorry it was so darn late, but we got there in the end.

Also Alice, my agent. You are a star.

And James Weston Lewis and Kate Grove, the artist and designer, for the wonderful cover.

LIGHTNING MARY

ANTHEA SIMMONS

WINNER OF THE MIDDLE GRADE STEAM BOOK PRIZE

One stormy night, a group of villagers are struck by lightning. The only survivor is a baby – Mary Anning. From that moment on, a spark is lit within her.

Growing up poor but proud on the windswept Dorset coast, Mary faces danger to bring back valuable fossils to help feed her family. But tragedy and despair is never far away.

Mary must depend upon her unique courage and knowledge to fulfil her dream of becoming a scientist in a time when girls have no opportunities. What will happen when she makes her greatest discovery of all . . . ?

9781783448296

CUCKOO
SUMMER

Jonathan Tulloch

Summer 1940. As the cuckoo sings out across the Lake District,
life is about to change for ever for Tommy and his friend Sally, a
mysterious evacuee girl. When they find a wounded enemy airman
in the woods, Sally persuades Tommy not to report it and to
keep the German hidden. This starts a chain of events that leads
to the uncovering of secrets about Sally's past and a summer of
adventure that neither of them will ever forget.

'A ripping wartime adventure and a love
letter to Lakeland's farms and fells'
Melissa Harrison